GETTING OVER HOMER

GETTING

OVER

HOMER

.

MARK

O'DONNELL

ALFRED A. KNOPF
NEW YORK
1996

THIS IS A BORZOI BOOK
PUBLISHED BY ALFRED A. KNOPF, INC.

Library of Congress Cataloging-in-Publication Data
O'Donnell, Mark.
Getting over Homer / by Mark O'Donnell. — 1st ed.
p.   cm.
ISBN 0-679-44590-0
1. Gay men—Fiction.   I. Title.
PS3565.D594G48   1996
813'.54—dc20   95-44016
                                        CIP

Manufactured in the United States of America
First Edition

to Homer,

despite everyone's advice

but really,

to Ann Close,

the founder of the feast

So quick bright things come to confusion!

A Midsummer Night's Dream

"Hey, these wisdom pills you sold me taste like shit!"
"See? You're smarter already."

Old Joke

CONTENTS

I MY, YOU KNOW, LIFE

1 My Dilemma   3
2 My Name   10
3 Dead Old Dad   16
4 Give Me Puberty   20
5 Blind Date with Destiny   25
6 The Salivation Army   30

II HOMER

7 Homer at Last   37
8 Trespassing in Paradise   45
9 The Vise of Vice   55
10 An Unwatched Pot Boils Over   67

III THE ODYSSEY

11 Greetings from Lake Stupid   83
12 The Lost Weeknight   90
13 Dear Anxious   93

14 A Dark Night of the Soul on the Town   100
15 The Sibling Circuit   110
16 My Double's Mate   125
17 Melting   131

IV   TEDDY

18 The New Year's Baby   137
19 My Lover, the Virgin   143
20 Policeman, Save My Child   149
21 A Triumph in a Teapot   155
22 Awful Young   161
23 Cry, Cry Again   163
24 Progress!   175
25 Cookie Fumes   179
26 Last Licks   185
27 All for Now   189

I

MY, YOU KNOW, LIFE

1 : MY DILEMMA

The punchline of the cartoon, of course, is that I'll probably do it all again. I can't help it. I'm a beauty fool. A hope dope. Hans Christian Monahan in—no, make that Hans Christian Monahan is—*The Prisoner of Hope.* In relentless 3-D and wraparound color! I haven't seen this epic all the way through, obviously, but I assume in the end I become bitter and weak enough to escape.

Meanwhile, though, I'm still hope-stricken. Even in that terrible dragged-behind-Time's-chariot stretch between Homer and Teddy, after that Christmas tree fire surrounded by strangers, I told my friend Lloyd that I had to believe life would improve later, and Lloyd, who must have been sick already, but I didn't know it, said that if I believed it would, then I was living in a Fool's Purgatory. After I figured that one out, I said at least that was better than living in a Smart Guy's Hell, but it scared me. For one thing, Paradise at any IQ was not on the menu.

Still, my secret bank machine code is L-O-V-E. I changed it to F-A-I-T-H for a while after Homer left me—I thought that would be healthier, since faith isn't supposed to really expect anything—but then my wallet was stolen, and when I got the card replaced I just went back to L-O-V-E. Anyway, when it was

F-A-I-T-H, I kept punching in L-O-V-E out of habit and getting nowhere with the machine. Actually, you're not supposed to tell anyone your secret bank machine code, are you? But see, that's my problem. I'm too eager to share, to commune. In bed I even cross my feet and hold my own hands to simulate sleeping with someone else. Plus it braces me for waking up in the morning.

What I still haven't figured out, in the great greenish gray scheme of things, is whether I've had more Communion or less than other people. I'm not talking about that limp plaster poker chip Sister Scholastica used to tell us would drip blood if we received it insincerely, I mean that fourth-dimensional feeling of being with other people happily. I don't want to pity myself, but if in fact I have had a lonely life, I think I should be told. On the other hand, maybe I'm a lucky bum, with all the sweet skirmishes and sibling solidarity I've had, and my song that people still whistle, and I just aim too high in expecting sublimity to be constant. Maybe I've done really well, and greed makes me pretend to be dissatisfied, as if acting deprived could get me extra portions. I'm a victim of song lyrics there, and TV commercials, and pornography. They all act like fulfillment is just a doorbell away. Or worse, they eat theirs in front of you. And with TV or porno, you are by definition Left Out.

It is possible, though, that I've actually known true love. I'm just not sure. You tell me. Just because I'm a songwriter doesn't mean I have professional access to answers. It's a paradox in a way, and in a way, it isn't. I might as well tell you the whole arguably beautiful ordeal. It's one of those coming-of-middle-age stories. A *bull-dung*-whatever. *Lost Labors Loved. My Rise and Fall and Rise and Fall and Subsequent Meditative Lateral Motion.* I know I'd sure like to tell you. Or to tell anyone, frankly. After all, those who can't repeat the past are condemned to remember it.

· · ·

As I said, it all boils down to that desire to Commune. First of all, I am a twin—Communion points there. People have always assumed there's magical telepathy and closeness involved, and I've always treasured their envy. I figure envy is the best measure of anything's worth. You already know Red, my twin. You'd see him (or me, actually) and say "Grogan!"—because he was Grogan on *Here's How!* for years. He *is*, I should say. That show will be in syndication forever, *in perpetuity throughout the universe,* that's actually how his contract reads. The entertainment magazines always referred to his character as "the affable barfly." You remember, Grogan was the unemployed one with the endless supply of Irish folk sayings that were supposed to solve problems but were just mystifying. "A man in love is a rabbit in a sack." Stuff like that, though I sort of get that one.

Anyway, Red's witness has certainly seemed to verify my theory of reality, as if he and I had crash-landed on Earth by being born—five minutes apart, like a meteor shower—and we're gathering data for our home planet. Aliens are always identical looking, aren't they? At least they are in sci-fi, which is all we have to go on so far, even if it's all made up. Non-twins in reality, in, what would you call it?—in sci-non-fi—they seem stranded, they have to figure it out on their own. I at least feel like I took two paths, and then reconnoitered. I Had Two Brains. I got Jukebox Earth's marathon hit parade in stereo.

On the other hand, we've had the same strain as civilian brothers, and Red has made it to marriage—that's a co-anchor plus some profound accessories—so he's ahead in the Communing department. Actually, he got married on *Here's How!* too, at Grogan's long-delayed christening. Ha ha, an adult being baptized at his own wedding, two sacraments at once. So Red's been married twice, once in reality and once in pop culture. And boy, is he stable, at least for an actor, so it's reassuring to have his dry land nearby, however occasionally rainy it gets, but it's also a reminder that I'm the one still dog-paddling in the Sargasso.

I may overestimate marriage, though—idealizing what I can't have. Homer was ultimately more mirage than marriage. Lloyd used to point to this cheesy gift-shop mock sampler he had hanging in his tiny apartment that read *The other man's ass is always greener,* with a picture of a naked babe in faked embroidery, and he said it was his secret mantra—*Others Aren't Happy Either*—though he didn't seem to get any inner peace from it. I know, even for the willing lover, it's hard to commune. With any relationship there's that imploding double bind of two people slowly colliding, sharing the secret of their willful Inner Brats. Marriage, that conclusive crown, is the outward symbol of maturity—and, like attending ultraviolent movies, it's a test requiring it.

But still, I'd always hoped spouses could at least become synchronized, so they could age abreast, be discussing the same scenery. Fully cordless Siamese twins by temperament. You know, mutual adoption. The question is, are twins, or lovers, or, while we're at it and since I don't know how they're matched up either, figure skating partners, two halves of one thing, or two versions of the same thing? Or just two more things, period?

One twin I met that disastrous time I went to AA—I'll explain later—said twins are just siblings with special visual effects, a neck-and-neck struggle without the usual age difference as a buffer zone, and the only fun of it is for others, perceiving it. His problem, or anyway, his starring problem, seemed to be that he and his twin had fought (over an inheritance, I think—I do remember he was an auctioneer) and didn't even speak. I'm grateful for people who are palpably more fucked up than I am, but I found him spooky. I don't understand people who don't speak to someone. I speak to everyone, even if like Homer they don't speak back. I'm speaking to you, and I hardly know you. But as I said, I'm a goon for Communion.

My second Communion plus: I have had virtually Vulcan mind-melds with my friends. We really open our four-chambered lockers, even if (my second minus) there hasn't been sexual air lock in those relationships. I'm a platonic Don Juan: instead of sleeping around, I joke around. The Sexth Dimension—it's the wild card in life's game of Go Fish, isn't it? It's destabilizing. The nitroglycerin in the love cocktail. I can't resist, though. I'm a sap genetically, like those absurd courting grouses on nature series, like any gamete-packing male—a slave to that little tall man downstairs who wakes up before I do. Like I said, I'm a Beauty Fool. (We had this French-Canadian art teacher in high school who used to enthuse over drawings she liked by saying in her accent, *"Zat is beauty-fool!"* and Red and I joke that whenever one of us is addled by sexual desire, we're being a *Beauty Fool!*)

Anyhow, in this famously tough life, love may be strictly extra credit, but it's my quest. Like Lloyd, I mean, Ulysses in my musical *Odyssey!*—I don't suppose you saw it—I want to get through the scary stuff to a safe haven and warm arms. I keep thinking I'm going to find sexual closeness like everyone else has, though Red keeps pointing out that everyone else hasn't, that I'm falsely suspecting others of venereal happiness. I hate to sound pessimistic, but I can't help believing there are happy lovers out there. I just pray I'm wrong.

Also—last on the Communion checklist—I'm tied for the youngest of a dozen kids. Again, you tell me if a big family makes me more isolated or less than, say, an only child, like my college roommate Dana, whose parents knew what he was majoring in, but criticized it. It did feel like a boardinghouse sometimes, our Monahan Manor, as my sister Bridget always called it in her secretly insurrectional deadpan. But, I must say, you never knew who to be jealous of, and it's great to know a whole crowd of people who understand exactly what you're talking about when you bring up Mom. We were Cleveland Family of the Year twice, too—that unified us—once after Dad was killed and once after Jock was. That made me unwisely associate self-sacrifice with a free dinner to follow.

Mom used to say we were the Kennedys without the money. That was her center, that we were the finest family in walking distance, but it wore us down, because she didn't like us to have problems. Too aware of what problems lead to, I'm guessing now. When Judy the Beauty canceled her engagement to the Libido from Toledo (we thought he needed a matching nickname), Mom carried on like it was a royal divorce, even though she secretly disliked him too and they hadn't even set a wedding date. Mom disapproved of selfishness, of the *spoiled*. She rated psychiatry as a vain variation on a pedicure, and she insisted that allergies were the self-indulgent fantasy of the rich, and forbade us to have any. So, when I had that first troubling crush on Duane Klack, I figured she didn't want to know.

Still, compared to the Lannigans next door, whose nine Pepsi-for-breakfast greasers were constantly being arrested for vandalizing St. Vitus's, or for shoplifting paint at Surplus City in order to vandalize St. Vitus's, we were at least outwardly shipshape. We were by default the class act on the block, where a social gathering's success was rated by whether nobody took a swing at anybody. And, one communing value of big non–Kennedy families, even the Lannigans, is that you learn complaining is pointless. It's like trying to get room service in the Black Hole of Calcutta. My rich roommate Dana used to fight with his parents during semester breaks because they had only two cars for three people. There was always ice cream in their freezer, but not always the flavor he wanted. Then years later he joined a cult. Now he eats gruel on a commune. I wonder if he was jealous of my big poor family, with our tribal survival vibe.

When I used to ask my older brothers to let me play football in the alley with them, though, they always joked that I could play Left Out. They didn't know how left out I felt, especially knowing that something was different in me, something weird and unforgivable, at least in Catholic Cleveland. I guess they were just joking, but in my anxiety I gave it the disadvantage of the doubt. I was the bottom of the pecking order, and when the frustration had been passed down the bucket brigade from eldest to youngest, there was no one for me to disgorge it on, so I had to accept de-livery and just berate myself. Low man on the scrotum pole. The brick stops here.

Even Red grabbed that five-minute gap to claim Older Brother powers, the way there's only a fraction of a second be-tween Olympic Gold and Zip. That may be why I want my true love to be a little younger and smaller than me—though Lloyd snidely said that was a symptom of my suppressed heterosexuality. But again, whether it would be to protect him or dominate him, to promote or exploit, you tell me. I'm seeking something sweet and pure, but in order to fuck it. I guess I'm not the first person who isn't sure if love is generous or selfish.

2 : MY NAME

You're probably wondering about my weird name, and where you heard of me before. I am actually a Trivial Pursuit question. Trivia may be big, but that doesn't help me, really. You don't get paid for achieving triviality. My biggest hit was when I was eleven—"Love Is the Answer." Well, the official title is "(Life Is the Question,) Love Is the Answer"—you remember it?

> *Life is the question,*
> *Love is the answer.*
> *Life is a dance,*
> *and we are the dancers.*

Well, that's enough of that. Okay, it doesn't rhyme exactly. I was eleven years old, all right? It was the willfully childish late sixties, right before I hit puberty. In a way, that's my problem now—I can't fake it now like I could then. Once you've actually loved, it's trickier to write about. In fact, once you hit puberty it's hard to get anything done.

What happened was, the song won a contest sponsored by *Vistas.* It was that kid's magazine. And, somehow, Sonny LaMatina (you know, "Rainbows Incorporated") found out about it and recorded it. You'll recall he was always doing whimsical hippie things like that, like giving that Concert for the Trees out in Wyoming—no audience, just trees. He even had me and Mom flown to New York to wave from the audience on *Ed Sullivan* when he performed the song with Sylvia St. Cloud and the Harlem Rehabilitation Choir. New York was thrilling, like a too-loud record, a playground without supervision. After the show, when Ed shook my hand and told my mom, "You must be very proud of your boy," she said, "I'm proud of all my children equally." You have to give her credit there, but at the moment I wanted her to concentrate on me.

She was determined not to play favorites, see. Like, I certainly wasn't allowed to splurge on my royalties, it would have been unfair to the others. Whenever anyone asked her why she had had a dozen kids—and they didn't even know about the miscarriages—she always answered, "I didn't expect any of them, but I wouldn't trade one of them for a million dollars." And we always chimed in with "Oh? Which one of us is that?" You'd think after the first few times we pulled that, she'd change the wording to "*any* of them," but she had her set way of saying things, and she continued to walk into the joke, like Margaret Dumont and the Twelve Marx Siblings. In the hospital, at the end, she'd start telling long, pointless stories we'd all heard a million times, and when we'd say, "Yes, Mom, we know, the First Job story! *Mr. Baum said, 'You're as smart as a Jewish girl!' and gave you the job!*" she'd smile and nod and, even in pain, still tell the whole long story again anyway, including what she wore—her only dress—while we'd be mad with boredom as well as grief. That's where a large family comes in handy, though, sharing the grief.

Anyhow, my first hit record. That's how you'd have heard of me, unless by some chance you saw *Odyssey!* off-off-off- and deep-beneath-Broadway. The lucky thing with the record was, they let me use my nickname on the label: *Blue*. Blue sounds corny now, but in the Day-Glo sixties nothing was unmistakably tasteless, and it sure beat Hans, which is what I had. The children's room at the Carnegie Library was called the Hans Christian Andersen Room, and there was an awkward painting of him hanging behind my mom's desk, that must have been her inspiration. She named all the kids (Dad never interfered, or so my eventually oldest brother, George, says), and she started getting fanciful at the tail end. I guess once you figure in all those additional confirmation names, she had run out of saints. Hence my youngest older sister, Louisa May: no one meeting her thought of *Little Women*—she just felt like a comic strip hillbilly, what with the middle name May, and she went for Lulu, which wasn't ideal either, if you're not an heiress. If you're poor it just sounds crazy. The older boys tried Loony on her, but she resisted, unlike Bridget, who actively embraced Bridge-out. Lulu's come back to Louisa, now that age has made it fit her.

Anyway, I read a child's biography of Andersen and somehow got it in my mind that Mom was telling me I was a weird-looking misfit whose only refuge would be fantasy. She may not have meant that, but she was always offering the literally shaky defense for my seeming struggle that I had had the smaller birth weight, that Red had weighed eight ounces more. We'd both been born a month early, but I was the only one who seemed to continue to gasp for air, and people always told us apart in photos by my frightened, deer-in-headlights eyes, which invariably glowed Martian red in color shots. I think Mom wanted me to be help-less, I was the last outpost of her Empire. No wonder I later loved Homer's thinking I was powerful.

Basically, nobody calls me Hans Christian. Almost everyone calls me Blue, and when George wanted to tease me he called me Blooper or Boo Hoo. Homer called me Big Shoe, but that was later and unrelated to Ed Sullivan. The family nicknamed me Blue partly because it was convenient to tell us apart with different color clothes, and Robert Louis got the red hand-me-downs and I got the blue ones. Which came first, whether the colors influ-enced our tempers or were chosen to match them, not even Mom could ever explain. Anyway, she didn't like conversations about psychology or motivation. She always suspected such talks would lead to one of us trying to get out of a household task.

Whatever the reason, I used to make crayon drawings of dancing elves and animals wearing clothes (to be fair to myself, I was just imitating all the old books we had inherited from what Mom called the library's Discontinued Line), whereas Red favored marauding dinosaurs and exploding Nazi airplanes. One time I drew some giraffes in party clothes kissing, and that made my mother uneasy. She asked me not to draw kissing. She never asked Red not to draw explosions, but I guess this is a timeless complaint.

And again, after Judy won free piano lessons for being Miss Junior Cleveland, I asked her to teach it to me—the piano seemed so elevated and pure, humanity without its faults—but Red asked for a harmonica, because his proud fantasy was that he was a hobo, or a jailbird, or one of the wounded at Guadalcanal. At Halloween, I'd dress up like a dutiful clean-shaven Union soldier, and he couldn't wait to dirty his face with burnt cork and put on his Rebel costume. We'd play cops or soldiers in the back alley—which did look like bombed-out Europe—plotlessly and eagerly shooting each other, practicing dying over and over, rolling in imaginary final paroxysms, even—or maybe especially—after Dad and Jock were killed. We both loved swigging from our canteens and hiding. Red would announce he was the Expert on Explosives brought in from Headquarters. I always preferred to be the medic or the cook, though all I could dispense in either case was chewing gum. I guess I wanted to prove I was good. Once I said I was from the Danish Underground, trying to solve things peacefully. I didn't really know what undergrounds did. I still naively hoped things could be negotiated.

Another possible factor in our divergent sameness—Bridgeout and Judy were in charge of baby-sitting us, and out of boredom, I guess, they'd race us against each other and place small bets on the winner. Once they even got us to jump off the garage, though I can't remember if it was a race to hit the ground first, or what. Luckily, Red wasn't hurt, he hit the lawn, and I was just stunned, and after I regained consciousness, Bridge-out gave me money not to tell Mom. Again, maybe that's my problem, I jump off high places and hope for positive reinforcement.

Blood-red-haired Bridge-out, always reckless and wild mouthed—how she ever lived with Raj for even a minute still astonishes me—must have coached my twin better, because he charged around fearlessly, whereas strawberry blond Judy the Beauty wanted me to be her doll, and she criticized me for not doing what she told me to, like sitting perfectly still for her Living Statue game while she talked on the phone, or practicing the quaint piano exercises about Jolly Milkmaids she thought were so sweet. Judy was Miss Cleveland Tool and Die, and a runner-up for Ohio Tomato Queen. That was her version of ambition back in what was a more limited world. Bridge-out always hated Judy's beauty contest forays, as the curvaceous good girl who happened to sing "Danny Boy" as a borderline sexy love song. Judy sang well enough to pursue it without the swimsuit parade, which Bridge-out resented ahead of her time, but in our boardinghouse family every member was free to follow his or her own superstitious gambles on bliss.

Anyway, my name. I tried never to use my official name. One of the many problems with it was that new teachers would call me Hans Christian, and ask about Denmark, and I'm not Danish, even though I came to want to be, as if I somehow wasn't white enough. In *National Geographic,* Denmark looked like pure escapism: innocently small and out-of-the-way, cleansingly blond and cheerful, all Tivoli and dessert, and I wanted to be clean and happy and safely out-of-the-way, though namelessly sensing I was shy for a reason made that seem impossible.

Even though no one ever acknowledged it frankly, I guess everyone knew. It was certainly bad for my image that teachers always said, "Hans Christian—like the man who wrote the fairy tales!" and Nick Spurgeon in the back of the room would start snickering and repeating *fairy* under his breath. Or even when they called me Blue, Nick would smirk behind his cupped hands, "He *did*?" One Christmastime they showed the old Danny Kaye musical *Hans Christian Andersen* on television, and the next day a group of older boys started chanting, "Hans Christian Monahan, Monahan the Fag!" Of course, it's possible they were just accidentally, randomly right. They called each other fags, too, when they annoyed each other. And in puberty's boot camp, they were all unwittingly, desperately dependent companions.

And again, Red lucked out because no one found anything odd about Robert Louis as a name, or even connected it to Stevenson and *Treasure Island,* or for that matter *Dr. Jekyll and Mr. Hyde,* which still would have been fine, those are macho books, as family books go. Even *A Child's Garden of Verses* never gets bathetic like *The Little Match Girl.* For a while in junior high Red even encouraged the use of Babalu as a sort of hip contraction, and all I could find for mine was Hanker, which may have been apt but I didn't want to advertise it. Once I complained to my mother that my name was confusing and she said, "Only to small minds. Great minds will appreciate it." She didn't seem to realize I had to take gym class with small minds.

There were a lot of laughs at Monahan Manor, don't get me wrong—dinner table Three Stooges reenactments and jungle sound-effect contests, lard-popped popcorn and wisecracks at lame TV horror movies, pile over fests on the tiny strip of lawn between our house and the Lannigans', doo-wop singing led by comical Conal, the piles of picture books I now realize Mom must have pilfered from the library—but again, there was a paradoxical isolation, too, all talking at once, Mom always surrounded, like our tired tour leader, and again, our duty, for her sake, to be just fine. And always, that absence where Dad should have been, and the guilt that this Jesus-like—only more verifiable—good man I couldn't see had died so painfully.

3 : DEAD OLD DAD

If you're from Cleveland, the story's as familiar as the Mr. Jing-a-Ling murders or the Cuyahoga River catching fire, or at least it used to be. Violence gets painted over by new violence, I guess. It's a busy world. But I don't know what I actually remember and what I've just picked up from the autumnally yellowed clippings since then. Basically, he was shot when he walked in on a candy store robbery and intervened. He was off-duty, he was just stopping for a candy bar, that was the ironic, damning virtue of it all. His father and brothers had been drunks, and he'd sworn never to touch alcohol—he was the white sheep of the family, but he was big on candy. Mom always said, "If only he didn't have that candy bar habit, he'd be alive today."

She had to act proud of him, but I think she resented his leaving her holding the bag—the formidably big bag. He was a cop, I don't know what she expected—exemption from circumstances? Still, people always murmured at me how wonderful he was, what a sweet man he was, and his self-sacrificing image preoccupied me, like the beheaded martyrs in our catechism, as an icon to live up to and a loss to atone for.

Those were the days before little people filed multimillion-dollar lawsuits. When Dad died, and then Jock, Mom just accepted the pension and the press coverage stoically, brushed up on her Dewey decimals, and went back to work at the library where she'd worked before she met Dead Old Dad. After all, these were people who'd shouldered the Depression and World War II without getting any restitution for Mental Cruelty. In the eighties, when that actress sued that director for nicknaming her Cookie on the set, Mom shook her head and said, *"Spoiled."*

My eldest sister, Ellen, was just out of high school—Jock and George were older, but men weren't expected to care for people back then—and she gave up a music scholarship from the Knights of Columbus in order to hold the family together in shifts, like a wartime factory, till Red and I were old enough to understand the sins of Breakage and Pilfering and so could be left unwatched. She jumped ship and got married right after Red and I reached seven—the age of reason, says the Church, when you know what Sin is. In those days you got married in order to leave home. She must have resented her stewardship, she was always on simmer, her voice as ominously level as thin ice, though she never yelled or punished us, and the only hint of her frustration was the occasional evening when she'd go up to the attic with her violin and we'd hear torrents of Russian cadenzas leaking down from the chilly, box-strewn aerie where she chose to sleep, just to be temporarily free from the figurative elbow knocking below.

Jock was still a police cadet when he lost control of the car he was driving and was killed in the crash. For years I thought he was in a patrol car, chasing someone, but it turns out it was his own car, after a party. He was pursuing himself. Or fleeing from himself—who knows? Ellen says she suspected alcohol, but it was never discussed. Closed casket. It was his way of getting out of the house, I guess. All I remember now is his long, smooth face, like a teenaged Easter Island statue, only instead of harboring some secret Answer, he seemed to harbor some secret Question—the troubled heir, the eldest as sacrificial lamb, or worse, as chairman of the workforce, impossibly tall and remote at the opposite end of the family. To me he was Superman retreating to his Fortress of Solitude, contemplating the basketball hoop in the back alley, alone in the gathering dark, waiting long seconds before invariably shooting a basket that didn't even touch the rim.

Then George, the Acting Eldest, self-consciously short and flippantly crew-cut, but still a dutiful Mass-goer, really wanted to be the next family cop. It was his obsession, like a procession of saints in a shooting gallery, but Mom put her foot down. Nobody wanted to push the point, then. Her bereavement was her perpetual trump card, and at the time we didn't even know about the horrors of her childhood. Anyhow, I remember a late-night argument, and George shattering a glass on the floor after promising to find some non-shot-at profession, as if obedience required a hydraulic geyser of personal will expelled elsewhere. Maybe that's why Jock drove so fast. Anyway, I think that's why George was later so frustrated at his job. He felt trapped in Waste Management, not to mention being second choice for eldest son. And, that may be why he loves singing those old Irish revolutionary songs, they're safe bits of rebellion, imaginary guns. Anyway, I must have been only four or five then, and the shattering glass thrilled me, even though I knew it was supposed to be serious. Passion looked like a great you-must-be-this-tall Thrill Ride. I wanted to break a glass, too.

And throughout all this I was just tumbling back and forth in the crowd, the extra who would be featured, and everyone dying made my loneliness seem selfish. Dad rejected me by being dead. My older brothers rejected me for being strange and small—or so I imagined. Maybe they were preoccupied by their own secret adolescent panic. Worst of all, once puberty privately unveiled my desires to me, I rejected myself.

Even Red had to retreat from me sometimes just out of self-protection at my drowning quality, as if I might humiliate him in the schoolyard by mentioning the Jolly Milkmaids or *The Magic Flute*. He used to cringe and say, "Don't talk that way! Don't walk that way!" even though people always marveled at how alike our voices and manners were. It's like the way you hate the sound of your own voice on a tape recorder, or the way you think everyone in the photo looks good but yourself. I did fear Red's disapproval, since his antennae were my only contact with a reality closer than mere clanking real life, but as the world revealed its natural currents to us, and schoolyard anxieties receded, he and I both got used to me. Well, you decide if we have.

4 : GIVE ME PUBERTY

Anyway, I'm getting to Homer, but first, my pre-Homeric love history. Or sex history, depending on which historical theory you buy.

I wonder if treasuring songs has hindered or enriched me. Virtually all songs are singing commercials promoting love, except maybe "Old Man River," which is more of a public service announcement about life's general misery. Even torch songs sell the glamour of the one pain you volunteer for. In music class, the other kids were indifferent as we sang "Juanita, we'll wander together, to the vale where the oranges grow. . . ." It was just more multiplication tables or pledges of allegiance to them, but I was excited—Who's Juanita, she sounds hot! Wow, a vale, cozy! Oranges, mmmm! Songs were feelings turned into places.

And as the youngest of a dozen, I had a lot of grown-up activities trickle down and over me, like additional half-lives, so all the music the older kids listened to filled my ears and made me aspire to romance and heartbreak, the great house beyond the vestibule. Ellen went at the classics like a prizefighter, George relished the sexy anger of Irish songs about Bold Fenian Men and how My Aged Father Did Me Deny, guitarist Kitty had her Derry

Down Diddle folky folderol, and Judy was always trying out some Wrapped Up in Moonlight song on the used piano Sister Scholastica gave her. Even Mom, generally so purposeful and inconsolable, would relax with a bedtime boilermaker and wispily sing along with Lawrence Welk, as he and his starchy drabs performed euthanasia on some potentially healthy melodies.

For a while Red and I shared a room with Sean and Conal— Red thrilled to the cramped double bunk beds, because it was like living on a naval destroyer—and Sean, the ranking elder, who lives alone on a tiny island near Seattle now, liked absolute darkness and a softly playing FM radio all night. He'd fall asleep to it, but I'd stare into the void as echo-chambered pop singers gently announced how ecstatic they were, or else how their world was shattered. Even now, the sound of Johnny Mathis unnerves me, because I associate it with absolute darkness and the solitude of sleeplessness, not to mention the secret, boundless, uninformed hope of prepubescence.

They also say religion affects your sexual behavior, like learning to share or to love spanking. We were perfunctorily Catholic at best, or worst, and I don't think I can blame my emotional problems on nuns the way everyone else on Earth has, Catholic or not. We went to public school, and Jesus and Mary were never mentioned at our house, though every bedroom did have a crucifix. I think Mom was just observing the technical requirements there, like with fire extinguishers She didn't seem to think much of the stultifying geezers who presided at St. Vitus's, and when I first got the picture I wasn't the marrying kind, and suggested to her that maybe I'd become a priest, she clucked, "With *your* mind?"

I used to take the glow-in-the-dark crucifix that hung in our room and hold it right up against a burning lightbulb so it would store up light and glow that much brighter in the dark, and then I'd sneak into a closet to watch it shine, but I wasn't sure if that was glorifying Christ or torturing Him. Mostly I knew it, I mean

He, was just a story, because even an amoral zombie can rise from the dead, and tricks like multiplying loaves and fishes have nothing to do with doing the right thing.

We did have Sunday catechism. It started out simple, with us drawing the Creation (starry night for me, explosions minus Nazis for Red), then the animals in Eden, and for the third class, family members for whom we were grateful (I drew George, Sean, Conal, and Red—I left out Jock, I knew that might upset Sister— and inadvertently labeled it MY BOTHERS). Then we were supposed to draw our idea of heaven, and Red was criticized by Sister Scholastica for including King Kong and Marilyn Monroe in his illustration. Heaven has no animals, especially imaginary ones, or suicides, especially sexy ones. Finally we advanced from pictures to words, and had to trace the half-invisible dotted letters spelling I AM SORRY. I didn't quite grasp what it was I was supposed to be so sorry about, but that made me even sorrier.

All right, I'm getting to my sex life now, though not with others. I was always the last one to use the bathtub water, but one benefit of being last was that I could luxuriate, and in that now incomprehensibly comfortable state before hormonal desire, I'd lie submerged in the tub—I was still that small—and, idly, raise my stiff mushroom penis and groin above the surface of the already-gray water, like an unlit island lighthouse on a murky sea, an intimate Atlantis emerging from the waves in curious adventure, only rising like newborn Venus instead of sinking in disaster.

I don't remember any nudity but my own. My sisters were scrupulously modest—especially Judy, despite her wearing swimsuits onstage—even after backyard hose fights, when they'd need to strip off their wet clothes in the basement. I didn't know what to look for anyway, though the curves of bikinis in sniggering television skits, or at Judy's pageants, were inevitably disturbing. I had no guidelines to such sensations, though, and had to guess at their meaning, like when you hear Beethoven's Fifth, or should I say David Rose's "The Stripper"?

It's not that I didn't find women beautiful, I did, but their curving forms were abstractly inspiring, like Bryce Canyon or a perfect chambered nautilus. I wasn't galvanized like the other boys when a *Playboy* centerfold was passed around, all unfamiliar pink mountains in the mist, but once the yin hit the yang, I did get involuntarily warm at the dancing sideburned delinquents when they showed *West Side Story* on TV. In response to this apparently incompatible inner universe, I decided to be the most wholesome kid there ever was. Wholesomeness was my fetish. A golden smoke screen. Ultimately, I was student council president. It got that bad.

Mom never brought up the facts of life, see, and when I had my first wet dream I was afraid I had gotten a punitive illness for my bad thoughts, because the elusively worded entry on sexuality in the medical encyclopedia at the library said venereal disease featured a white discharge. When I told Red I thought I had gotten venereal disease from a dream—and I certainly didn't mention the dream was about Duane Klack—he rolled his eyes and said I was Too Weird for Belief. Somehow his friends had prepped him more fully than me.

Once I figured out masturbating, I used foggy sports-page photos of friendly high school guys that I stored in an old copy of *Heroes Every Boy Should Know* (battlefield self-sacrifices, mostly, Nathan Hale, Father Damien, that crowd). I just imagined them liking me to the point of orgasm. It seemed normal enough to risk Mom's discovery, since even regular boys love their idols. The only time she ever walked in on me, luckily, I wasn't using visual aids. All she could think to say before retreating was "Blue, get hold of yourself!" Not the greatest choice of words.

For a long time, I didn't even get the concept of conception. At first I had thought women had babies because of something magic the priest did during the wedding ceremony—I didn't know about illegitimacy—and then I thought maybe they conceived through the breasts, since everyone else was so excited about them. Then at a basement party at Nick Spurgeon's they showed a soundless Super-8 porno loop that lurched in and out of focus like JFK's assassination footage. The man's penis looked like a little purple gangster, and the woman's vagina like the helpless eye of some forlorn sea mammal. Needless to say, it was depressing, and, without sound, it might as well have been flagellates flailing weightlessly on a microscope slide.

I still haven't gotten to sex with other people yet, have I? I mean, I haven't talked about it yet. I took my student council vice president to Prom—she had hinted it behooved us—but my good sportsmanship was not the same as chemistry, and she sighed through the weekend like a princess under house arrest. And I simply avoided myself in college, concentrating on my solo album and studying the *Odyssey,* and besides, being gay at noble Leeward would mess up your chances to be president later. Only, finally, in New York, where you can go insane for all anyone cares, or, just as uselessly, sane—did I acknowledge desires more specific than my generalized childhood theory that *Love Is the Answer.* A few painful misfires, a few wonderful misfires, and then Homer. Homer, who cried with happiness when I carried him up to the roof of his own building he'd never even been on. Homer, who then left me alone with the ocean.

5 : BLIND DATE WITH
DESTINY

Despite, or maybe because of, their love of music, my brothers always mocked my sappy hit—"*Duh!* is the question and *Duh!* is the
answer! . . ." Even Judy found it didn't work for her act ("Too
general!"), but the royalties—Mom kept them in the bank so I
wouldn't get a disproportionate sense of self—let me pay for my
own and Red's college expenses, which I think mortified Red at
the time, though now it's about one hour's income for him. Since
I wasn't dating in high school, I had time to perform Chopin for
mental patients and try to grasp mitochondria, so I got into Leeward, that brand name of Ivy League rectitude, but hitchhiker
Red cut a swath through the nymphs in his art class and neglected
his schoolwork to play harmonica in a half-kidding jug band,
The Unemployables (yes, he named it). So, he had to settle for
Buckeye State, where he always claimed over the phone to be
majoring in either recess or mixology. Actually, he majored in
history—invasions, explosions, Nazis again, you know. Buckeye is
the college where the ten students were killed in the crush after
rushing the field at Homecoming, and there was that fraternity
pledge who died from being fed bourbon through a funnel.
Somehow Red found it reassuringly all-American. He barely

graduated there, too—he said his degree was *Thank You Thank You Laude Laude*.

People always pointed out that he was easygoing and I was more tremulous. Well, sure, he could relax. His desires were applauded at every turn, by our brothers, by television commercials and comedians' routines, by church sermons and street hoods—whereas, I wasn't wired to get it, I was a pariah waiting to happen.

Leeward, with its stained-glass dorm windows and complacent portraits of its alumni presidents, fills its students with an obligation to achieve great, tasteful things. As a sophomore, wracked by its atmosphere admonishing me to be famous—my roommate Dana actually knew the Kennedys—I paid to record an album of my own, voice and piano, a dozen songs as sweet and similar as whole-wheat donuts. I rushed into it, really, I was achieving too hectically, and used up a lot of my royalties, and it only sold about a thousand copies. Hearing it now I realize I was a shaky performer, and it was badly managed.

I should have been suspicious of any record producer based in New Hampshire—Lonny Graven had no other visible clients, and even the technicians at the studio used to trade Yeah Right looks when he snifflingly blamed an unspecified meeting that always made him late to sessions. Reviews, if the local free papers' free association counts as such, derided the finished, or should I say, released, work as sophomoric, which was really too easy, don't you think? And I should never have called it *Cornfields*. I was walking into the critics' hands there, but it seemed so beautifully wide-open Woody Guthrie populist at the time. After *Rolling Stone* passingly cited *Cornfields* as "John Denver without the danger," Sonny LaMatina—who'd been floundering in self-parodic sitcom cameos himself—sent me a bouquet of extra-thorny roses and a note reading, "Welcome to the clubbed." Getting through the album's failure was my first taste of workaday adult disappointment, my first transport to Always Always Land. But even that is nothing compared to love failure. That's like getting fired from your evenings and weekends.

Time flies, or anyway, pours, and Red and I both ultimately landed in Manhattan, by default as much as determination, a blind date with destiny. After four years apart we didn't have to fear over-dependence on each other anymore, or schoolyard smirks, and we found a cheap walk-up to share. It was like pup-tenting way out of sight in the backyard, family made simple. Mom, of course, shook her head that we didn't have specific ambitions or techni-cal skills like the older boys, and even after the *Ed Sullivan* ap-pearance, when I had said I wanted to be a songwriter, she had whispered in my ear, "Remember, grown-ups have to make liv-ings." Megan, who was forced to take steno over harp, used to refer to her as Mother Discourage, but Mom knew it was a steno over harp world.

New York is a demanding yet dismissive mistress. I eked by on my evaporating royalties and on occasional cabaret jobs accompa-nying self-conscious chorus girls pretending to pay tribute to Rodgers and Hart. I tried to get my musical version of Homer produced—not my yet-unmet Homer, antiquity's—while Red hooked up with some illegal Irish aliens and got a cash-only job as a moving man. It was his version of youngest-son defensiveness. He knew it would impress George, that he was working hard labor outside the law, secretly sneering as he sweated moving a Bronxville professor's collection of boulders or a lawyer's suspi-ciously well-polished antique torture devices. It was an innocent time for both of us, and whoever got home first took the bed and the latecomer got the couch, unterritorial sharing we'd picked up in the socialist state of Monahan Manor.

Red would have his illegal buddies over to play poker, which I tried but never enjoyed. They say poker is destiny in miniature, and that's my problem with it, it's too frighteningly like life, every-thing's a gamble requiring nerve. People fold. But these guys were more *Iliad* than *Odyssey* fans—they sought victory, not security.

If I was increasingly aware of my identity, I certainly didn't dare try dating men with Red there to represent the family's dis-may. Later on, the mad therapist who wanted to massage me while I described my sexual confusion suggested I was in love with Red, but if I'm not my type, why would my twin be? And besides, sex is a substitute for love, not the other way round. Well, usually.

Red certainly knew I was castaway on a desert isle in the sea of sex, but the borderline older brother in him preferred me to be inexperienced, and when I told him I thought I was gay, he asked if what I really feared were adulthood's mortgages and child-rearing expenses. He didn't know gay people had complicated finances, too. Hollywood was still ahead.

And here's how that happened. On an office move Red guilelessly befriended a playful Texan woman who turned out to be a cast-ing director. Jeannie Howe—she discovered Atom Boy, Gordon Wells, but you should like her anyway—enjoyed Red's self-deprecating charisma, and the fact that he didn't think of solicit-ing her for work like everyone else who got near her. Eventually, unexpectedly, she called him in to audition for a foot-odor-pad commercial—P.S. He got the job. Remember? He looks hurt as his TV wife says, "I love my husband, *but*—" Then he was a reg-ular guy at a fancy restaurant who'd rather have Pavlik's kielbasa. He started making big money as poor clods.

Then Jeannie set him up to audition for a sitcom set in a bar-room, a little thing mankind now knows as *Here's How!* "His energetic lack of ambition gives him an appealing quality on-screen," he said she'd said. He turned on the phony brogue we'd always used at home to enact dim-witted laziness, or rather, to hide it in plain sight, and she laughed loudly at his callback so the producers would think they were discovering him. I wonder if she was already in love with him.

Red had to move to Los Angeles, but he insisted on finding a place with no pool. A pool would have been *spoiled,* and anyway, he didn't exercise. The show was a surprise hit, or as surprising as anything could be you've spent a million dollars to promote. Weirdly, there my co-zygote was in the tabloids, making extravagant I'll-Eat-This bets during breaks on the set or arriving at Awards with voluptuous supporting actresses from his network's other shows. I had my first throat-constricting taste of adult solitude—or freedom, that sounds less Boo Hoo—but Red's newfound fame and my newfound obscurity sharpened that taste, as being denied his comfortable sexuality had tortured me as a teen.

Our celebrity status had shifted, but I was determined not to be Cinderella's galled stepsister, that would just poison my own water supply. We still had our weather-beaten love and combat veterans' mutual respect to navigate through the ego confusion. We each still needed to take the other's temperature to take our own. And luckily, we saw good fortune is as much a punchline as bad. Actually, we were mutual consultants, the aliens gathering data, and foremost, we sought to do what is "classy"—that is, not to act *spoiled,* to do whatever is the most upright thing to do: what would Dad, St. Augustine, Lincoln, or, in Red's view, Sinatra have done?

But his shooting schedule—professional and erotic—was consuming, and for the first time, he got hard to reach. So I got out of touch with myself.

6 : THE SALIVATION ARMY

Freedom is an open sky but also a yawning chasm. New York is caffeinated, it enthralls, but it makes its thralls edgy, prevaricative, free to be selfish in its vastness. It's a million-horse town. New Yorkers can't Be Here Now, they're more I'm Supposed to Be Where When? No one escapes from Fun City's networking party, where they dance entranced to ambition's tarantella. Everybody's funny and nobody's happy.

What happily surprised me, though, when I started going to bars, was that people saw me as tall and broad shouldered (thanks for the genes, Dead Old Dad!). They didn't know I was Boo Hoo the runt, that the prince was an enchanted frog. In fact, for the first couple years, whenever anyone even paid me a compliment I'd write it down in a little notebook when I got home. I labeled it *Comfort for Cold Nights,* though when I got it out and read it after Homer left me, it made me more sad than happy. Stuff like "You can be my master anytime!" and "They'd love you in porno!"

I got voracious then, the way we'd all wolfed our food as kids, afraid it would disappear. The Salivation Army, Mom called us, and all her boys were speed champions at the Clean Plate Club. I came out and gorged with relish, my own extravagant I'll-Eat-

This bet. I was maddened by the siren song, a swine at Circe's. I followed my penis around like a dowsing rod looking for moist land. I had good sex with dumb guys, dumb sex with good guys, and, occasionally, good sex with good guys who weren't looking for a relationship. Distracted, self-doubtful young people seldom alight simultaneously. At last I was a cocksman like Red, only secretly, serially, and fruitlessly. I was popular and lonesome at once, for the second time, only this time I was Student Council President of Whoopee.

And meanwhile, with the increasingly decreasing savings from "Love Is the Answer," I worked for a couple years on my, if nothing else, ambitious musical version of the *Odyssey*. Man's search for home, if not meaning. Unlike the *Iliad,* which is all warfare, this had romance and travel. I loved its combination of classy mystery and borderline absurdity—any life you know?—and finally I rented a little space down in the East Village called the All Mammal Theatre, to mount it myself. It's one thing to write a song, you only need to record it, but with a musical you need twenty people to go crazy with you for two months, and not always for pay.

Legends should be lavish, but we had to try for stylized starkness. You can't really do the Cyclops properly on a low budget, and I could never get his song right—singing monsters are inevitably goofy. And the offstage (tight budget, remember) sirens' music was never irresistible enough. Ulysses had only three crewmen—it's the smallest possible number that will suggest a crowd onstage. Without money we did all the magic effects with masks, which actually was classy and not, as Mom might say of fancier trappings, *spoiled*. Telemachus seemed to preoccupy me—the faithful but unknown lost son, who must wait to prove himself. Anyway, he had the most songs.

That's how I met Lloyd Harris. I'd seen him improvise the roles of Superman and Albert Einstein in a basement revue called *The Earthling Hour,* and thought he might play brains and brawn at once. He came in to audition—huge, barrel chested, and wavy haired enough to be Greek—and when I asked him if he'd read the script, he said, "Yes, I've read the, as it were, script, and I have a few suggestions about how to fix it." He could make his voice low and *mag-nif-i-cent* onstage, but in offstage conversation he was always snippy and sardonic. The body of Superman, but the mouth of Lex Luthor.

"First of all, you open with Telemachus missing his father. What are you, hung up on boys? Why not open with Penelope, so you can frame it as a love story?"

"Well, that's how the actual *Odyssey* opens."

"Well, the actual *Odyssey*'s in Greek, but you've felt free to play with that. And come on, you should have someone as Homer himself, the *Odyssey* is about narration!"

You seldom see an actor expressing interest in parts of a play that don't involve him, never mind having read the classics, and I cast Lloyd as Ulysses, even though his manner was more snide than wily, because his voice and physique were strong, and his angry quality seemed to work for the part, though at the time I didn't realize how angry. Also, no one else was willing to work with an inexperienced director for the bus fare I was offering.

Lloyd always mocked the show offstage, calling it variously *The Idiocy* and *The Oddity*, but he played it straight onstage, a marvel of cynical professionalism, and in one song, "What Is Home?" he seemed genuinely involved:

> *What is home? Is it all inside my heart?*
> *Is it in another heart? Is it a place?*
> *What is home? From the world a world apart,*
> *Is it a land, a hill, a house, a face?*

You get the gist. I cast my friend Milla Korones—I'd accompanied her nightclub act—as the only woman, both Circe and Penelope, as well as Calypso and Athena, plus the offstage sirens. She was double cast for supposedly experimental but actually economic reasons. It was a lucky bit of misfortune, because it gave the play resonances four different women wouldn't have. Milla was voluptuous but unsteady—half-Russian, half-Greek, so she was torn between the urge to kill herself and the urge to kill others. She was very tall and busty, like a figurehead on a ship—dizzying, really, you'd think she'd rule the waves, but not many men wanted to attempt to scale her. Amazingly, it's the assholes who leap at well-built women, not the regular guys—and few knew how self-conscious she was about it. She played Circe not as a sadistic witch but, with her dark, saturnine saucer eyes, as a furiously despairing woman, disgusted with men, who simply lets them be themselves, a hostess resigned to guests behaving like swine.

I don't know why I let Lonny Graven, who'd also moved to New York, produce the show. He'd done such a terrible job on my album, but I had no other connections, and there was a perverse kind of compulsion involved, like going back to a lousy restaurant, hoping if you give them a second chance, God will give you one. Anyway, I was already over my head directing, and he was supposed to manage the Reality part. For opening night, though, he made sure we had a full house by recruiting a busload of derelicts from a downtown shelter. With the audience wandering up and down the aisles, wailing, and addressing, if not always the actors, their long dead rivals, it was hard for the critics to concentrate on the stage. Imagine an earthquake during your screen test. That's why you never heard about it. That, and we had no advertising budget. And I guess there is that chance the show sucked.

After *Odyssey!*'s abysmal closing, in our mutual depression, I admit, Milla and I tried sleeping together a few times—talk about experimental theater—but we were speeding the wrong way down a one-way street. She thought she was complimenting me when she said I reminded her of a man she'd loved who committed suicide. Let's just say she was too tall for me, too, and for her in her isolation I must have been beef jerky in a midwinter cabin. Also, I felt like Lloyd playing virility onstage. When I dared to tell Red about it, and that it felt like acting, he responded, "I don't want to hear the details, but, hey, for a lot of *straight* men it's an act."

See, after that two-scoop fiasco of the musical and Milla, I had an extralong-distance call to Red. "When the right one comes along," he continued, "you won't have to act, you won't be able to help yourself. A man's gotta screw what a man's gotta screw." That was his way of announcing his acceptance of me, I guess. And when I found Homer, I couldn't help myself. Of course I also hoped he was to be the repository of my *classiness*, the focus of my energies for promoting happiness on Earth. People don't always like being repositories, though.

II

HOMER

7 : HOMER AT LAST

Our birthday—that sounds funny, doesn't it? *Our* birthday—is October thirtieth. Yes, the night before Halloween. Mom always said she had wanted to beat the holiday rush. In Cleveland it used to be called Beggars' Night, when teenagers panhandle from door to door, a lazy street-clothes parody of trick-or-treating. On the night we turned thirty, Red had promised to call me at seven my time to talk and catch up. Ten o'clock, ten thirty, and he hadn't called, and he wasn't at his home or his office. It wasn't like him to break a promise. I panicked and felt abandoned by my best friend and reference point.

I wanted company— I was turning thirty, for God's sake—and it was Saturday night besides, and a full moon. The combination pulled me out of the house like a marionette. I went walking under the moon, which was glaring irresistibly, like a gigantic hypnotist's eyeball, and in my bath of bathos I suddenly remembered the opening of the *Inferno:* "In the middle of life's journey, having lost my way, I found myself in a dark wood ordering some Italian drinks, oh, martinis, say . . ."

I headed for the dark wood—in this case, the Loading Dock, a dark dive in the meatpacking district that, in the age of AIDS, provides a safe momentary whiff of Eros or, anyway, Pan. It was hard to tell who was wearing Halloween costumes, since it always looked like Halloween in there, with studded black leather and military gear from no specific nation. I downed one beer and got a second as a prop, and watched the cruising, blank-faced men waft by like Dante's dead Italian friends. They were merely provisional company, of course, shades in that netherworld between solitude and contact.

They always say you find love when you're not expecting to, which is either a reassurance or a warning. It was just midnight, I remember, because the digital clock above the bar read zero zero zero zero, and suddenly, there before me was a grinning imp in a leather jacket, moon faced like Buddha but curly haired like a ranch hand. I never remember Homer entering rooms, he seemed to appear like a genie. I felt an involuntary catch in my throat, that ecstatic *Mmah!* chefs make when they've sniffed the exquisite on their ladle.

I looked over my shoulder, like the vaudeville clown I apparently really am, to see if he was actually grinning at someone else, but no, he was grinning at big, blond Hans, unaware it was ludicrous Boo Hoo. It wasn't that he was lovely, though he was certainly the fabled nice guy in a dump like this, but his eyes sparkled with a charged sense of fun this kind of grave, windowless fun spot generally forbids.

"Hi there, Stretch. Now don't laugh— my name's Homer. Can I buy you a beer?" Wow, an elf who granted wishes. It was an odd sensation from this smaller man, though, a baby offering a stranger candy.

"My name's Blue. You sure have an appealing drawl."

"Blue, like a hound dog! Well, I'm from a place you never heard of—Petty, Texas. *'Stranger, beware!'* "

"Why?"

"I mean, that's my hometown's motto."

"Ah! And it is small?"

"Boy howdy! Geographically, mentally, spiritually. First prize at the church raffle was a gun. I had to come here to look for love."

"That's like going to the Sahara to swim, isn't it?"

He tried a Bogart-like lisp. "Yesh, I was misinformed." Then he reverted to his sunny Texan accent. "But I'm still hopin'!" He handed me a beer and winked.

I obligingly sipped the bottle he gave me, though I still had one. When it overflowed onto my chest, one of the black-jacketed hulks nearby giggled, but Homer put a reassuring finger to the spot.

"I see you're an excitable boy." He spoke softly, drowsily winsome. His hooded eyes nonetheless shone, like those of a high-spirited person who just got out of bed.

I hadn't found myself in old movie steam like this before. "Well, it's the beer that was excited," I stammered. "And it was that way before it got to me."

He traced a slow circle on my chest with his finger, feeling the hair beneath my T-shirt. "Oh, you underestimate your powers."

"Whoa! You have powers yourself! Are you a sorcerer for a living?"

He smiled, removed his finger, and spoke more straightforwardly, to demonstrate his ability to exist on the mortal plane as well. "Actually, I guess I am! I work for Antonio Maraschino, the party planner?"

I'd read about Maraschino in gossip columns and seen him advise TV viewers about how to entertain royalty more effectively, unrolling his dubious Italian accent like a carpet salesman showing you a counterfeit rug. "Sure. He's the one who designs galas for socialites and big executives?"

"The very, very, very one. He takes them out to dinner, and I do all the work. I drape rooms in silk, spray-paint books gold, hire the mermaids, dress the band like cannibals, that kind of thing. I provide the icing on the icing! I'm the fun broker, the liaison between money and funny. They aren't celebrations so much as displays, though. Show windows of success. They hire me to create a fun setting that also says, 'Boy, Am I Solvent!' Basically, the design concept is *Looky!* These people spend more on a party than most people do on a house. It's sad, and silly, actually."

His rapid commentary fetched me even faster than his flirtation. That incongruous first name was the only evidence that Homer was once a hayseed. "You must be the slickest thing Petty ever produced."

"Well, we had a serial killer!" He looked down bashfully for a moment, and then startlingly refocused his eyes on me. "Some people do expect me to be slightly dim, with this backwater *drawwwl,* but that way I can then sweet-talk them into really good deals for Antonio."

"You do talk sweet," I said, Silly Putty in his hands.

"I walk sweet, too," he purred, and brushed against me. "Would you and those long legs like to take a turn in the moonlight? I'm just a block away." Had I been mistakenly cast in the lead of *Happy at Last?* He was that supposed oxymoron, sexy and sharp, and of course it thrilled me that his name was that of the poet who'd preoccupied me for years. It seemed so predestined, but maybe the Greeks' faith in that influenced me. Modern science knows Chaos rules.

The romantically antique cobblestones gleamed like a junkyard of crescent moons under the streetlights as we walked past the still-dark meatpackers'. "Have you ever read any Homer?" I asked.

He turned up the stupid in his drawl. "What? A bunch of dead fightin' furriners! I'll take the *Looove Boat!* Leastways that's Amurrican!" he joked. But still, it showed he knew the plot.

"So, were you named after your father?"

"Maybe. I don't know. I'd have to find out who he was first."

I'd found it's better to seem not to get a joke than to laugh when someone's serious. Homer saw my halted expression and grinned. "I'm just teasing, I know who he is. I just wish we knew where he is!" He grinned and paused again. "No, in fact I do know. He writes me from prison." I actually stopped walking. "Blue, you are so much fun to confuse!" He grinned again, and nestled into my side, kissing my arm as it gathered him in. "No, my dad's a nuclear scientist, a smart guy like you. He, uh, he worked on the H-bomb!"

His tiny apartment was a mock-religious spook house of lovely, unsettling southwestern folk carvings of angels and devils, and Homer mischievously claimed to be both. He lit several candles—"Hey, they're the poor man's fireplace!"—and their organically shifting light made the impassive wood virgins and skulls seem to be living, but lost in thought. No one I'd dated in the past went to the trouble of candlelight.

"You know," I mentioned, "I haven't thought of this in years, but I, I mean, we had a hand-me-down teddy bear somebody had named Homer—my mother's joke, I'll bet—because he'd lost both his button eyes."

Homer pulled me close and sang, "So, I'm your teddy bear, your lost toy! Your Rosebud!" We kissed, and his lips tasted like milk and pepper, both cozy and provocative. "You know, I did a party for Ruma Volat, the columnist, and she told me that in real life Rosebud was the nickname the real Citizen Kane gave his girlfriend's pussy!"

I had never discussed pussy with anyone, unless you count overhearing Nick Spurgeon recite it to himself over and over in eighth grade, but here it wasn't jarring, he made it sound like an invitation. We kissed more, submerged in it, and I impulsively lifted him into my arms, fireman style. He sighed and murmured, "I love . . . this."

"I love your loving it," I answered. His little, lonesome body made me feel as strong as Dad must have wanted me to be. Carrying him from couch to bed, I was the strength giver, not the victim of circumstance.

I like kissing during sex, call me greedy, but it completes a circuit, an electric illusion of circular fulfillment, immortality somehow racing around the positive and negative endings of two of life's batteries. And, whoa, the comfort of the penis in its nest is nature's closest simulation of intimacy, whatever that is—Communion, closeness, the soul kiss of bodies, the key in the ignition, Ulysses at Ithaca, Daddy's docked! *Honey, I'm Home!*

And Homer was so avid and abandoned, slavish and energetic, not sickbed clumsy or mindlessly selfish like the worst of my previous partners. Now it was my turn to be mindlessly selfish, and I liked it. The cracked wooden glorious sorrowful saints surrounding us looked down, impassive in the writhing candlelight, and either they understood everything or they understood nothing. Time passed, and our lovemaking coincided with the ever-busier dead-of-night roaring and gasping of the meatpackers' trucks on the slick cobbles below, the calliopes at the carnal carnival.

"You are certainly one red-blooded American boy," he said grinning at one point. We lay in a welter of sheets like nearly drowned sailors washed ashore.

"Oh boy, so are you!" I said, trying to conceal how thrilled I was at the unaccustomed ease of this dreamland.

His face fell to a deadpan. "No, Blue, I'm cold-blooded." He stared at me for a second, and I felt panicked, as if God had changed the channel. Then he grinned again, ecstatically, my beloved freed from the spell, and his eyes sparkled. "Blue, you should see your face! I'm just teasing again, and you are so earnest about everything, like a little boy!"

"Speaking of earnest . . ." I used this as a means to bring up a subject that dampens a first date like a heart attack on a game show. "I should have told you sooner, but I'm in very good health, I'm HIV negative."

He looked sheepish, and stared into his pillow. It's customary to offer your name when a stranger reveals his. "I . . . Blue, I haven't been tested. I'm just afraid to. I feel fine, though." Heaven had a hitch.

43

"Well . . . We were safe, I used a Love Sock."

"Do you still want to stay?" he said, and the preparation for rejection in his voice touched me.

"Man, I'd love to. You are worth the—well, it's not a risk if we're careful. And I bet you are negative."

"It doesn't make a difference to you?"

"It might with someone else. Not with you."

"What a nice *earnest* thing to say . . ."

I told him I thought he should get tested, but I never mentioned it again—I thought that was the classy choice. By late morning his mysterious chambers had become as sunny as a farmhouse in a flashback, and his statues more like playthings. His digital bedside clock read one, one, one, one.

We idled arm in arm, and I perused his rough-hewn treasures. One carving showed Adam and Eve embracing in the roiling flames of hell. I always wondered what had happened to them. Homer clutched me and wailed in falsetto, "We're sorry we fucked, all right, Lord?"

His humor and ease were my long-sought *classiness* itself. "I can hardly wait for you to meet my twin."

"Mmm," he reflected. "It's nice to know if I accidentally break you, I'll have a backup."

"Do you have any brothers or sisters?"

"Probably." He laughed. "No, I'm an only child. Only me, only Homer." He said it like an apology, and glanced up at a beautiful grandfather's clock.

"That's a beautiful clock!" I said supportively. "Was it your grandpappy's?"

"Ooh, in a way." He smiled. "I told my ex-lover Derek I needed a watch, and he sent that over. He's always doing stuff like that. Well sir! I'd love to have you stay and assault me some more"—he smiled drowsily—"but some people are taking me out to brunch."

"Oh, good for you. Being honored on Halloween?"

He winced, like it was a joke he was tired of. "No, actually—yesterday was my birthday. The big three oh. I didn't want to bring it up because it might have seemed to put pressure on our first date."

He didn't just say date, he said *first* date. And what's more, I had found my astrological twin.

8 : TRESPASSING IN PARADISE

Red finally phoned that afternoon. It turned out he'd been given a surprise party on the set, and the staff didn't think about the twin part when planning it, and besides, I was a continent away.

"They whisked me off in a limo to this place so trendy it hasn't even opened yet, and I couldn't quite break away to phone," he explained sheepishly. "I feel awful about wasting your evening, but I got lost in the moment. And, I have to admit, Blue. . . . It was a little on the wonderful side."

"Well . . . It's okay." I would have been angrier if I hadn't had a wonderful night, too. "In fact, I went to a party myself." I re-tooled the truth in my eagerness to share it with Red without making him squeamish. "I met a great guy, one of those droll Texans, he's named Homer Winger, you'd dig him."

"Oh good. So was it a party in your honor?" He hurried past the meeting-a-guy part.

"Well . . . Ultimately, yes."

When I phoned Homer for a second date, he said, "Sounds grrr-eat! But let's play a little game. Meet me at the Loading

Dock again, but pretend we haven't met before. Pick me up all over again. And wear dark sunglasses if you have them."

When I went up to him in the bar and played the gruff stranger, Homer grinned, but then faked fear and backed into the wall behind him. A poster there read, PUNISHMENT IS ITS OWN REWARD. "A-Are you gonna make me?"

It seemed wonderfully funny, and not presumptuous, for me to advance onto him, and kiss him as if forcibly. For our third date, Homer asked me to meet him at the Loading Dock and pretend I was a cop arresting him for delinquency, a fantasy that pleased and unnerved me with thoughts of Dead Old Dad. I was getting spoiled—*spoiled,* the thing Mom damned but the state I dreamed of—by Homer's fanatic subservience, every man's dream of a personal and personable slave. Even though he was saucy and managerial by day, he played my helpless devotee in the dark, riding, not running the roller coaster. Lloyd pressed me for details and sniffed that I had control over something at last.

At Homer's suggestion, I pretended to be his disciplinary sergeant, his high school coach, and even a tourist at a border-town brothel, with him as the desperate boy of the streets.

"Treat me like the trash I am," he whispered.

"You're not trash," I answered. "You're treasure."

"That's really nice," he said. "But that's not part of the fantasy."

I wonder now if he loved me, or a series of strange men. I would never actually hurt him. A Danish ballet dancer I'd bedded years before—to try to acquire Danishness, I guess—had wanted me to tie him up and beat him, but I just couldn't do it with a straight face. Volunteering for violence during sex is like going to art school to major in detention. One night Homer said his former boyfriend Derek the Oilman used to beat him, but when I offered consolation, Homer laughed and said he was just kidding, that Derek was a great guy. "I love fooling a smart guy!" he teased, literally rubbing my nose. He was prankish, and practical jokes can taste oddly of sadism, but if I was boggled from moment to moment, I was always sure of his brilliance and his need, so thrilling to find in one partner.

He seemed to fall for me, and went from chanting "I'm all yours!" at night to "I love being with you!" which is technically "I love you," there's just a small escape clause, loving the *being with* abstractly without involving the other party. I certainly fell for him, though I guess I was branding unborn calves on Expectation Ranch.

I knew I was getting serious when I started buying him gifts two or three at a time, knowing there would be at least two or three dates to come over which I could distribute them. And I was proud of myself, not knowing his HIV status, for standing by someone who might be in danger, or anyway being on standby to stand by, being potentially true when future false friends would walk.

We strolled along the twilit Hudson and watched used Love Socks float by. He lit more and more candles to ennoble our love-making, and even if I was his kidnapper or prison guard, I always brought roses. That's right, this is the Happiness Montage. Happiness is always shown in montage because it's a difficult sensation to reconstruct for more than a second at a time. It's a manmade element that quickly decays in the acid air of reality. Any man in Eden is trespassing.

He did occasionally have small aches and ask for a breather, and I was deeply impressed to learn that while working on a party in the Hamptons, he'd been in a helicopter crash that had drowned everyone but him. He was still recovering. It gave him a magic above and beyond his already tender light. Like Lazarus or Jonah, he gained the beauty of a victim and a survivor at once. And I could take the rescue from there! Plus, immigrant offspring me was thrilled that Homer was a Westerner, arguably a cowboy, he said his parents had *a ranch,* he was part of that deep, sweeping, profound natural American tradition whose longing music touched me so deeply. I'd consider my life a success if I'd written "Red River Valley."

It's also possible I was boggled not just by his country purity but by his added coat of magazine-perfect gloss: he kept fresh-squeezed orange juice in the refrigerator at all times, wore designer clothes that looked normal on him, and he surprised me with gifts, like a tailored suit from Needless Markup. That's what he called Neiman Marcus. "Big Shoe, I measured you in your sleep!" he crowed, as if the gift were another practical joke. "And let's face it, you are Sartorially Challenged."

Grooming was never a priority at Monahan Manor, and in any case it was too personal to discuss, and the only grooming tip I got at Leeward, for all its gothic preppydom, was roommate Dana suggesting I shave before I dress, so any resulting blood didn't get on white shirt collars. Homer, the puppy who owned his master, taught me tricks no one had ever bothered to mention to me—like how you can tuck the hidden underside of a necktie through its designer label, to keep it from flapping around, or that Listerine is not the mouthwash to use if you're going to be kissing someone. When I balked at his suggestion to get a haircut once a week, he said, "The president gets one every day."

"But I'm not a media figure," I offered.

"Well, you are visible to the naked eye."

After Lloyd met him, he said, "Well, I hate you now. He's smart, gracious, and perfect, so perfect he even acts easygoing so the perfect part doesn't frighten people. My theory: he's either Cute Made Man or time-released trouble. No hex intended."

Hey. Hex intended.

Little Homer Winger swept me into a sophisticated, almost hysterical world of relentless catered parties, moonlight cruises to promote new liqueurs or to celebrate acquisitions, convention-sized bar mitzvahs with cakes shaped like the Wailing Wall, last-minute helicopter trips—yes, despite his accident—and painstakingly perfect penthouses. Throughout, though, Homer mocked what he did while doing it well. "Can you believe," he'd confide, "this guy wants a red carpet unrolled for his arrival? Not for comedy—for pomp!"

For a gallery opening for a Swedish artist who made bronze casts of cattle torsos he himself had mutilated, Homer mischievously arranged to decorate the room with bloody cowhides and had the caterers serve barely cooked entrails and chocolate mousse cups in the shape of turds.

"Won't the guests be insulted? Or revolted, anyway?" I wondered.

"Oh no, Blue, they'll eat it up and say, Thank You, Dear! They're all so rich and nonetheless desperate, they want to show someone, strangers, that they're *good sports* as well!"

Homer trimmed busy people's Christmas trees for five thousand dollars a throw and filled swimming pools with bubble bath for forty-year-old socialites' "slumber parties." At one Park Avenue matron's birthday—I'd sometimes come along as Homer's "associate," he even charged them for me—every guest was given the choice of dressing up like a kitty cat or a Barbie doll, her favorite things, and given a free camera to take souvenir shots of the masquerade as well. Barbie dolls and plush toy cats were hung by the netful from the ceilings, a coming rain of windfall gifts for the party's end. Homer circulated beforehand, with a hair dryer, blowing hot air on the vases of fresh-cut white roses to make their petals open, because the hostess didn't think the blooms were voluptuous enough. "Big white arrangements" she'd repeated to him about the flowers, and Homer whispered to me, "That's my job in a nutshell—Big White Arrangements!"

He occasionally lost patience with his inefficient assistant Devon, who had what Homer called caterer's disease (being more status conscious and supercilious than the millionaires you depend on), but Homer was always as smooth and flirtatious with his clients as he was with me—"The first half of Success is Suck," he explained. I bore with it, because I loved knowing that this Delight Rampant would come off the field to me, that after all the gaudy panoply, he'd come home with me, trade his scepter for my arms.

I admired how hard he worked, but it unnerved me, too. "I'm in Workaholics Unanimous!" he joked, but he was determined to make more money each year than the previous one, grimly convinced the economy might collapse at any moment. "There is going to be a crash that'll make the Depression look like Sunday dinner, Blue. I don't want to end up out in the cold. It's an eternal tennis game for cash. It's an endless battle."

"Well, couldn't you find a relaxing tropical job somewhere?"

"No, Blue. It's a battle wherever you go. There are no tropics."

He was constantly managing parties for Japanese corporations thanking each other for the last party. Once one gives another a gift, it starts an endless cycle of gifts and receptions—like an arms race of generosity. He also accepted a commission to produce a gala for oil executives at the Kuwaiti embassy, and I was uneasy about it, though for no tangible reason. Homer argued, "Am I supposed to say, No, you're dubious? No, you're decadent? Or No, you're corrupt, and then lie down and die? Does that mean I shouldn't do City Hall pass-the-pork parties, or who-needs-it perfume launches, or socialite balls, or news-free press events, or NFL bashes? What's corrupt, anyway? Trying to make a buck? That's just trying not to die! Everyone's corrupt, then, Big Shoe! You love Art, but you do get paid for it! You can't judge who's innocent. Everyone is innocent in their own mind, and everyone is corrupt just by existing."

I asked him if his father had felt guilty about working on the Bomb.

He looked puzzled. "What are you talking about?"

"You said your dad worked on the hydrogen bomb."

"Did I? Oh yeah, that's right. Well—he didn't work on the whole bomb, just some small components."

Still, Homer claimed to admire my idealism and even my lack of credit cards. On the precipitously warm first evening of spring, he got teary when I brought him long-stemmed red and white roses, especially after I explained they symbolized the true blend of passion and sincerity.

"You see more fabulous arrangements than that every day," I pointed out.

"Yes." He buried his face in the blooms. "But this one has meaning. Those other flowers don't have a thought in their heads."

"Let's go up on your roof for sunset! Are you allowed up there?"

"I don't know, it never occurred to me!"

I picked him up, my stock-in-trade, I guess, and carried him up the two flights to his roof. The door to it was open, but no one else was up there as we looked out over the warehouse roofs and the Hudson, and the hazily idealized New Jersey beyond.

"It is some kind of nice night when New Jersey looks like a land of enchantment!" He beamed, took my hand, and then spoke with unusual gravity. "I want you to know, Blue, I'm thinking of branching off into my own business. I think I can do it." Then he added, with more familiar glee, "I'd call it A Business Doing Pleasure with You! What do you think?"

"That's great!"

"And I can take a lot of Antonio's clients with me! Hey! Why not? I do all the work anyway! And after some of the things he's done to me, I just can't forgive him, I shouldn't have to work for him . . ." It was suddenly one of his remote moments.

"What? What did he do?"

"Oh nothing, never mind him. He's a snob. A bigot. This is too beautiful an evening to let him affect it."

"So— Well . . . is there anything I can do?"

"I'll say! But not in this case. You just keep on giving me confidence." He buried his face in my chest as he had in the roses. "Oh Blue, I didn't think I could ever feel this way again! You've made me feel worthy and desirable! And no one's ever valued me in the way you do! Oh, listen. . . ."

He shyly started to sing, something he seldom did.

What is better than bread? Hope.
What is sweeter than wine? Thirst.
That's what I thought at first.

What is better than hope? Love.
What is sweeter than thirst? A kiss.
I went from hope to bliss.

Somewhere he'd found a copy of *Cornfields* and memorized a song from it. That took devotion. It was a love song written without experience, but it was probably the closest to a passable cut on the whole album. Taste points for Homer.

"I'm in love with you," he said.

"I'm in love with you," I rushed back, as if I might somehow still say it first. If you've been there, it's a nice there to be.

"Blue, this is the most important night of my life!" We gazed as the last red light abandoned the sky, and held each other. A man and a woman were doing the same on another nearby rooftop, beneath colored lanterns that grew more bright with the contrapuntal darkness. This was the life I'd been waiting to kick in. We slow-danced to music drifting up to us from somewhere below. At last, this was what music was like *along with* love, instead of *instead of* love.

The music suddenly got rockabilly, and Homer whispered, "How about a little rooftop Rodeo?" Sex with him made me believe pornography could be journalism and not fantasy.

Afterwards, we lay looking at where the cosmos would be if the city's glare didn't obscure it. "I'm so flattered you memorized that song," I repeated.

"Oh, I memorized the whole thing." He beamed and skipped to the end of it.

> *What burns faster than straw? Love.*
> *What is better than hope? Bread.*
> *That's all that can be said.*

I reviewed myself from a decade's distance. "Too bad I made it end so sadly."

"That's why I didn't sing the whole thing."

We went back downstairs, and as we passed his telephone table, Homer playfully picked up a piece of paper, a check, and waggled it in my face like a belle teasing her beau with a fan.

"Guess what this is!" He grinned. "It's the first installment of my settlement from the helicopter service! My Prize for Survival! To start up my business!"

He put it away, lit some candles, and poured two bourbons. "Mr. Jack Daniel. Lowbrow and potent. Like you."

"Is this what your folks drink on the ranch?"

"What ranch?" He seemed confused.

"I thought you said your parents had a ranch."

"Oh, right I didn't hear you. Yep. Except during Lent. Then they drink house brands."

"I'd love to see a photo of the people who made you. Do you have any?"

"Nope. We never had any taken, really." Now he seemed edgy.

"What's the matter?"

"Nothing. . . . Actually . . . Blue, my mom died when I was very small. Like, in a car crash?"

"Whoa! I'm sorry! But why didn't you tell me before?"

"I didn't want to depress you. I wanted to seem normal."

"Well, nothing's normal." This was a strange, serious variation on his Derek-beat-me jokes. "It's not your fault. And it wouldn't affect my feelings, why should it? Besides, I told you about losing my father. You and I are like mirror images!"

"I know, I know, but . . . I wanted you, and I didn't want you to think I might be weird."

I was mystified. "You're the most beautiful package God ever packed," I fumbled.

"Never mind," he said, and stared into the miniature flame reflected in his glass of bourbon. "Things are fine now, that's all that matters." He blew out the candles. "And I'm all yours, sir."

We made love again, on the liquor-lubricated Slope of Abandon, and we both chanted the recently released I Love You at climax. It had been a day I'd dreamed of all my life—but every day has its dog. In the middle of the night, sickened by the bourbon, I guess, Homer started uneasily shifting in his sleep and finally stiffened in waking and muttered, "I have to go deposit that check. The machine's at the corner."

"Can't it wait till morning?"

"Something might go wrong, it might get lost, I have to do it now." He had the blurry resolve of a sleepwalker.

"But like what? It's gonna blow away?"

"Exactly. It might blow away." He pulled on some loafers without bothering about socks.

"Well, wait, I'll come with you."

He never seemed to recover full consciousness as we walked to his bank machine, eerily fluorescent in the soft blue, leaf-hushed Village night, like a police precinct or all-night gas station, or a luminous shrine on a country byway.

"All-night banking," he mumbled as he received his printed receipt. "It never stops. Go go go. Go Go Boy. Satan never sleeps."

9 : THE VISE OF VICE

"I'm invited out to Derek's place in the Pines this weekend,"
Homer announced one June night. "It's a huge place. Why don't
you join me for some high-power relaxing? You can meet my so-
called friends."

"Will Derek like the idea of your bringing your new sweetheart?"

" 'Sweetheart?' You are such a lovable throwback to sentimen-
tality, Blue. No, Derek won't be there. He's working."

We went by seaplane to Derek's beach house on Fire Island,
first circling the gleaming skyscrapers of Wall Street, themselves
looking like well-dressed salesmen, gigantic, square-shouldered
robots of Commerce. *You like my looks? Buy my goods!*

At first, the Pines would seem to be a world apart from that.
The primal tang of sea air, the easy sprawl of underbrush, and a
simple wooden boardwalk above it, as if floating in midair, wind-
ing its way like the yellow brick road. It all invites simplification,
but its visitors make sure to bring marketplace anxiety along.

Derek's house was the size of a civic recreation center, and it
was furnished with the white couches and carpets that signal No
Toddlers Expected. I affected the abject brogue we used to use to

imitate sozzled Mr. Lannigan. "Someday, I swear to God, I am going to *work* in a house like this!"

Homer laughed. "Today only, Irish are allowed."

"That is one grand piano! Who plays?"

"Nobody. Well, you. I arranged for it so you could play if you wanted to."

"Oh, sweet Homer, you didn't have to! How on earth did you?"

"Hey, I'm a party planner. If you were a circus act, I could have booked lions for you."

"And all these fresh flowers! We're only going to be here for a few days!"

"We're only on Earth for a few days. Gotta have flowers."

In the kitchen, also an anesthetic white, one of the housemates stood meticulously dicing vegetables. The white counters made it look like surgery.

"Hi, Alden! How's bankruptcy going?"

"Great!" he said casually. "I'm making gazpacho for dinner. And Crawford's interpreting some chicken." Alden looked stocky and untroubled, like the plump, baby-faced execs I'd seen going margarita mad in their work suits at happy hours.

Homer cracked a tray of ice into a glass pitcher. "No one just has franks and chips out here. Designers never vacation." He poured a bottle of vodka onto the ice. "Alden, this is my friend Blue. He's a Leeward man." My credential, I guess.

"Hi! You're a designer, Alden?"

"No," he returned evenly. "I'm a bankruptcy lawyer. Well, I guess I'm designing in the scheming sense." He efficiently swept the decimated vegetables into a bowl.

"Yes, Blue, there's a lot of money in bankruptcy." Homer added tomato juice and put some glasses on a tray. He held up the empty juice carton. "Look, fresh-squeezed tomato juice! You don't get that in Petty! Come on."

We headed toward the rear deck. I felt a slight headache as we emerged from the cool interior of the house into the hot glare,

with the bracingly vast open beach beyond. An older playboy
type, whose very skin was somehow designer label, stretched on a
chaise longue, his eyes closed toward the sun, and a very young
man, perhaps a teenager, with a blond buzz cut and helpless eyes,
leaned at the railing pointing out the Atlantic Ocean to an in-
attentive puppy in his arms. His angular, starved schoolboy face
looked out of place on his bodybuilder's frame, like in those old
flip-books where you can put the head of an ostrich on the body
of a gorilla, or vice versa.

"*Qué pasa?*" Homer greeted them.

"Please," murmured the playboy, without opening his eyes.
"No Latino talk."

"Act glad to see me, everybody," Homer deadpanned. "I've
brought a tray of Bloody Marys just to make sure you are." The
drinks had so much vodka in them they seemed pink and anemic,
like a glass of water someone had been rinsing his bloodied hands
in. "Folks, this is Blue Monahan. Doesn't that sound like a dangerous drifter? Anyway, don't be frightened of him, he only
dresses like an anarchist. Blue, this is Mr. Crawford Z. Pike. You'll
never guess what the *Z* stands for."

Crawford didn't actually speak to me, he just smiled like I was
part of a parade in his honor and, with royal slowness, took one of
the drinks. Even in denim shorts, though I admit they were crisply
ironed, with his slicked, silvery hair and dry self-possession, he
looked like he was breaking the bank at Monte Carlo. "Crawford's in charge of the Old Masters," Homer explained. "At the
Met. He decides in what order they'll be presented—like seating
party guests!"

"Is the *Z* for Zebulon? Like the explorer?" I ventured, hoping to impress but sounding unsure to be more likable. Crawford
smiled and nodded. I guess his sunbathing required concentration.

The young man at the railing screwed up his face in distaste.
"Eew! Imagine having your head full of obscure facts like that!"

"And this is Phizz. He's Derek's new *sweetheart.*" Homer winked at me on that last word. "Phizz believes in airy, uncrowded mental lofts."

Phizz didn't hear; the edgy little spaniel kept squirming out of his grasp. He tethered it to the deck railing and sat with us.

"Fizz?" I offered to shake, which seemed to confuse him, but he may have sensed my confusion as well.

"You know, like Chaz for Charles? I'm Philip James, so, Phizz! It sounds preppy, don't you think?" He leaped up again and went over to scan the beach beyond the porch. "Just want to get a look at the competition!" he confided, appraising the trim young men who were passing on the beach in self-conscious seeming indifference. Like I said, the Pines is called a vacation spot, but Manhattan-style competition still prevails, the adrenaline of ambition, panic doused in spiked punch.

"I was at a county fair in Illinois last summer," commented Crawford. "Chicago friends took me. All those fat farmers! It was *disgusting.*"

"That's the irony." Homer grinned. "In this country the rich are thin and the poor are fat."

Phizz pointed to a sloppily dressed little man grinding a toe in the distant surf. "See that geekling there? You can't always judge a bankbook by its cover. His grandfather invented Technicolor. Every time anything's in color, he gets a royalty." Then he added, without adding anything, really, "He must have more money than . . . *God!*"

Everyone laughed like that were a fresh joke, to be sociable, I guess, or else the height of the income made them giddy.

Alden joined us and picked up a Bloody Mary tentatively. "Is there Tabasco in this?" He sniffed the glass.

"No," said Homer, and whispered to me, "Crawford and Alden have ulcers." The compromised glitter of City Mice at play. "They're not supposed to drink, really, but one step at a time."

There was a silence, as if everyone was reading the menu. "Are you still going to Rio?" Alden finally asked Homer.

"Oh, I'm always *going*." Homer sighed. "I just never quite go. Work work work."

"Rio?" It was the first I'd heard.

"Ohhh . . ." Homer squinted into the dazzlingly sunlit water. "I have a friend there . . ."

The dog whined, straining at its leash. Phizz interrupted the silence by noting, "So, I've been here half an hour and no one has said anything about my new baby."

"He or she is beautiful," Homer obliged him. "What happened to the Lhasa apso you had last year?"

"I just, I don't know . . . I got tired of it," Phizz offered. "But this one is for keeps."

"I can't believe I used to have a dog," Alden offered. "I could never handle the responsibility now."

The hot, consoling sun on my face made the slight conversation easier to take. Ice cubes tinkled like wind chimes. Phizz's dog seemed luckily oblivious to the string of pearls it was wearing.

"It's a King Charles, isn't it?" I sallied. "Like Nancy Reagan's?"

He beamed. "My spaniel is *related* to the Reagans'!"

A phone rang inside. "That'll be for me!" Homer sighed. "Work work work." He stood and went inside, and the languid group suddenly became animated, like the toy shop after the humans leave.

"I hear he's getting a huge settlement from that helicopter service!" bubbled Phizz. "I know you just met him, Blue, but poor Homer was in and out of hospitals and court all last year!"

"Actually, I've known him for about eight months." I guess Homer hadn't mentioned me.

"Anyway, it must be huge. What's standard for living through things?"

"He's come a long way in the world," Crawford, the tanned sibyl of the chaise longue, unexpectedly announced.

"Well, he's from a poor family, isn't he?"

"Well, his dad's a scientist," I pointed out.

"He was adopted, I got." Alden seemed to be reciting from a report his team had put together. "He doesn't know who his real parents were."

"I think he had parents," I found myself saying.

"He was like an orphan when Derek found him," Phizz went on. They were talking faster than I could listen.

"Orphan is an outdated word."

"Oh, Phizz! You're implying he was a hustler?"

"Well, kept, anyhow. Don't quote me."

"I hear he ran away from home because his father beat him."

"Well, if he was a teen runaway, he brought along a stylist."

Crawford spoke again. "I *said* he'd come a long way."

"He was a model for a while, I heard. I think I saw him in a porno movie. Or anyway, an ad for swimwear."

"Oh Phizz, I doubt that."

Crawford offered dryly, "Maybe it was some kind of conceptual modeling, where you don't pose for cameras, you do it secretly."

It wasn't my right to contradict them—I was their guest—and I was scared, for some reason. There followed a gossips' guilty doldrum I foolishly tried to fill. "I hear he killed a man once," I drawled, trying to make the joke Homer might have if he'd been there to defend himself. Alden and Phizz just stared, but then Homer returned.

"Derek sends grrrrr-eetin's from somewhere off Scotland." His drawl came through his attempted burr. "He's drrrrr-illin' for oil there."

"Did he send me any message?" Phizz asked.

"He said, 'Don't sell the house.' " Homer smiled, and winked at me.

"We're invited for cocktails at Cuddles's," announced Crawford.

Homer arched his eyebrows to signal mischief. "We refer to him that way because he's the least cuddly person you'll ever meet."

. "We should have a party here," said Phizz. "Then we wouldn't have to grope our way home in the dark on those . . . planks."

Crawford eyed him dubiously. "The word is *boardwalk*. You know this place is too small for a party, and there's no pool."

"Would your real friends care?" I asked.

Crawford eyed me dubiously now. "New on Earth?"

As we mustered to head to the party—by *mustered* I mean Phizz put on sandals to go with his Speedo—I took a break to use the bathroom. It, too, was a pristine, sunlit white, like an ideal room to be born in, and as I stood and peed, I closed my eyes to relish the soft breeze that was billowing the window curtains in my face. In my face? I suddenly realized the curtains had crossed my line of fire and I had drenched them with urine. This was not suave. I instantly averted my flow and hit a few guest towels before I'd curtailed myself. I called for Homer in a low, musical voice, and when he saw what had happened, he stood lost in thought for a principal's office second and then burst into laughter. He closed the door and kissed me lightly, like a teacher would, on the head. "You are such a . . . guy! My ape man from heaven!" he teased and took down the curtains. "They needed dry cleaning anyway." Of course they hadn't.

I took his hand to walk to the party, but Homer whispered, "Would you walk with Phizz, *Big Shoe*?" He used his spouse voice to ask favors. "The Getty just bought a painting Crawford wanted for the Met, and I'm afraid he needs counseling or he *just won't be able to go on*."

"Hey, I'm your helpmeet." I grinned, and he rubbed my forearm in acknowledgment.

The luxurious boats we walked past in the harbor had names like *Catbird's Seat*, *Wherewithal*, *Ain't Hay*, *Overtime*, *Arm and a Leg*, *Pretty Penny*, *Rewrite*, *Senior Partner*, and *Doc's Docked*.

"The SS *Excess!*" Homer called out and turned back to add to me, "Which one shall you and I go round the world in?"

"We won't need a boat for that!" I called back.

"Are you Monahan as in Monahan Chemicals?" Phizz asked. *How much did you say your name was again?*

"No, no relation."

"And what is it you do?"

"I'm a songwriter."

"Oh, that can be good," he tried. "I wish I had time for stuff like that."

"You know," I offered as Phizz's spaniel stopped to piddle on a piling, "as far as I know, Homer has a living father he gets along with pretty well."

Phizz stared at me. "Well . . ." He chose his words carefully, appeasing a madman. "I suppose such things are *possible.*"

Cuddles, a Texan who did something financial no one grasped, was the image of the fleshy, growling Boss, with a ravener's grin, the wolf's head on the bear's body. The furniture in his pool-blessed beach house was all intentionally weathered Protestant hunting lodge, *nouveau ancien.* The guests were uniformly fit, undressed, successful white men. Power as Porno and vice versa. Blonds with Bonds. Most of them had never met Cuddles, but their good looks made them his peers. Bodybuilding is itself a kind of materialism, pelf of the self, though some of them, even naked, seemed trapped in armor, lost boys overapologizing. I wasn't a millionaire, I was barely a thousandaire, and my body was more stubborn weed than cultivated. There had been wealthy students with last names for first names at Leeward, with furniture that time and not designers had weathered, but there the moral rustic setting and cafeteria dining had temporarily equalized everyone, and the ambitious were aiming for Westminster Abbey more than Beverly Hills.

The party cliques talked about antiques and spring collections, country homes and cupboards, and I felt the strange banality of beauty. Don't get me wrong, I'm aesthetic, I like things, I just don't like stuff. I didn't think I wanted a country house and things Ming, but something now gnawed—when in Rome, covet what the Romans covet.

Cuddles himself prowled around poolside, edgy and eagle-eyed, as if the party were an investment in danger of collapse if he didn't keep emptying the ashtrays. "Nice to meet you, Cuddles!" I grinned as he finally got near us, an hour after we'd arrived.

"Cuddles? What are you talkin' about?" His rough incomprehension, and Homer's momentarily panicked eyes, made me realize Cuddles was a nickname he'd never been told about. Homer managed perfectly and smoothly, though, like a master criminal explaining how the jewels got on his person. "Blue calls everyone Cuddles," he continued pleasantly. "He's in showbiz. Or else Babydoll. I'm Sugar Shack. Cuddles was the most macho choice, in this case."

He winked at me, and my near gaffe was suddenly his secret talent show. Phizz played along. "Ooh! Eric there can be Babydoll!" Phizz announced the obvious after others had seen it and moved on.

Eric, Cuddles's insignificant other, Venus to his Vulcan, Cuddles occasionally urged in one direction or another, as if the lost-looking redhead were a slovenly scullery maid or a fractious eight year-old.

"Go, that mesh shirt on Eric, it's awful," Phizz whispered "He looks like the catch of the day! What a fashion victim!"

Homer's expression was the mock-solemn one he used to make jokes. "No, I'd say he's a fashion *perpetrator*. And besides, he *is* the catch of the day."

"Hi, Eric!" Phizz had been caught looking at Eric and was now obliged to go chat with him, as if he'd meant to.

"Isn't Phizz an idiot?" Homer crooned indulgently, a good-natured man who faced facts. Still, I felt uneasy at how everyone out of earshot on this magic isle was routinely roasted. I decided not to mention his housemates' conjectures about his past.

"Boy, I sure think so, but I thought it was just me. How could your Derek go from a bright guy like you to him?"

"Well, the more powerful Derek gets, the less patience he has with being contradicted. And it took me a while to get bright."

Several other couples were mismatched in years, too. "I don't get the young man–old man deal," I said. I probably feigned too much unworldliness with Homer. "Though I guess I should be glad there's a chance for everyone."

"Them boys is social climbers." Homer smiled blandly. "They don't want lovers, they want *levers.*"

The noisy, crowded scene was joyless, the perfect bodies cloying in sheer numbers, assorted integers in the Empty Set. The guests all claimed to be on ecstatic drugs, but no one said anything visionary. Mundanity enters even a palace, I reassured myself, despite the endless blue ocean view and the limitless, even bluer margaritas.

"Chatter chatter everywhere, and not a thought to think," Homer whispered, anticipating my thoughts. Cuddles, or whatever his real name was, noticed Homer's whisper and must have suspected insurrection.

"Are you boys havin' a good old time?" he boomed suspiciously.

"It's so generous of you to have us!" I enthused.

"Even though I'm not blond," Homer added playfully.

"Bless your heart! You're blonder than some things," Cuddles kidded, but a cold glance escaped him toward a presumably uninvited Puerto Rican boy in a floral shirt. "Now y'all take some of this food home with you," Cuddles continued, indicating the colossal and nearly untouched buffet table. "I don't want Eric to have to clean it up!"

Homer smiled as Cuddles advanced to a new front, but he shook his head. "*Bless your heart* is code for *fuck you.* He reminds me of some other Texans I've known. So generous, to show they own you! So friendly, and so intolerant!" Then his face went ominously blank. "Cuddles did something to me years ago I just can never, never forgive."

"Wh-what was that?" I asked, though his titillating remark sounded oddly closed.

"I'm not going to say," Homer answered flatly, with a moral sigh that implied he was too classy to betray even someone he disliked. Again, I was slightly unnerved at all the people he couldn't forgive.

Crawford joined us. "That Deco poster is very valuable. He shouldn't hang it where the sun is going to bake it like that. It'll fade. Red is the most fugitive color."

"Fugitive?"

"Fugitive, it flees. It's the color that fades quickest with time." I thought of the ads in the window of the candy store where Dad was shot. True enough, the ice cream and potato chip images, and the smiling, outdated teen faces adoring them, had been sunburned to unappetizing, faint blues and grays.

The party began to disperse. "They'll all be heading home to make dinner, and then, in a few hours, they'll all do fresh drugs and head to the disco," Homer explained. Trapped in the Vise of Vice.

"All this scheduling. It's like a summer camp, or a monastery."

Homer humorously lifted his plastic drink cup to toast the scene. "Yes, and all the inmates have taken vows of Profligacy."

He pulled me close and swiveled us to the disco music that had been playing in the background. "And instead of Silence, a vow of noise! Lots of noise! Lots of distraction! Ee ha! Grab your partner! Promenade home!" We kissed, and I thought again of how he mocked what he also practiced.

The ball unraveled just as Homer predicted, but he and I went for a walk instead of returning to the house for dinner. His white, soft, living hand burrowed into the shell of my larger, rougher one. The setting sun happily shattered itself across the serenely inexpressive ocean. We walked along the beach as sunset turned to moonlight. It was in itself a trip through time, he and I together through change.

"Which house shall you and I live in?" he teased, as we passed assorted modern beach houses, winged, sleek, and outlandish like World's Fair pavilions. "I think we belong on Water Island, it's more isolated and familylike." Their lights receded, frail as tears, and we headed down the undeveloped beach into the pure darkness nature intended to keep man in line. The fishy breeze on our faces felt like honesty after the sophistry of party cigarette smoke, and the moon's splintered ribbon on the whitecaps provided the only flash of light in this unearthly—no, make that earthly at last—landscape. We lay in the dunes and made love; it was our own dark, private planet. Afterwards Homer humorously grabbed my clothes and ran away with them, so I had to chase him down the beach. I'd never run naked at top speed under the moon after something I loved before. It sounds satanic, but it felt closer to transcendence. When I caught him—as always, he made sure I did—we rolled in the water and kissed in the surf.

"It's *From Here to Eternity*!" I beamed with that happiness that can't help including disbelief at its own intensity.

"You got it!" he whispered. I realized he didn't know it was a movie title, he was agreeing to the trip. A few waves washed over us like we were playing dead.

"Call me a Booster, call me a Jaycee, Blue, but I believe we live on the most beautiful planet in the universe!"

"You're usually not so enthusiastic about organic life."

"I haven't always been this happy with it."

At last my life was resembling a song or, better yet, a commercial, which never ends in grief. "I wish we could have kids, Big Shoe, 'cause you'd make a wonderful father."

My blue heart was bright red, a Valentine red, finally. But then, red is the most fugitive color.

10 : AN UNWATCHED POT

BOILS OVER

Summer ripened, shaggy and careless, and Homer started leaving his clothes and paperwork at my apartment, a sign of stability in our relationship that thrilled me. The delight of his company became as natural a part of my life as eating and seeing, which are also loved ones easily taken for granted.

One night we went to a fund-raiser that aimed to refurbish the grand entrance of a downtown government building—the Lobby lobby. Despite its rococo purpose, the party was held in an ostentatiously austere SoHo loft, with guests whom Homer reported were the Power Gays. Those sound like kids' action figures, don't they? It was the Pines with clothes on, and the Caucasian sheen and razor-perfect grooming made me claustrophobic, since they all knew Homer (my beloved, not the poet) and none knew me.

Even in my Needless Markup suit, I was the klutz at court. Phizz, looking even more childlike in a grown-up necktie, admired the gold cuff links Derek had just sent Homer from Arabia. Derek's platonic yet plutonic gifts to Homer rattled me. The past is real, but it shouldn't send packages.

"I guess Arabs don't need cuff links!" Homer mused.

"And what has your *current* boyfriend given you lately?" Phizz thought he joked.

Homer used his solemn voice. "Phizz, Blue has given me the greatest gift any man can give another."

Phizz looked impressed, and turned to me. "You gave him a car?"

Homer played impatience. "Don't you understand anything?"

Some well-turned clubman whose name I hadn't heard put in, "Well, wouldn't a house be greater than a car?"

Homer smiled. "That's right. He gave me a house." Then he winked at me.

"No, no, it's a joke," I felt obliged to explain. "I gave him love."

"Oh," said the one I didn't know. "A joke. And that's the punchline?" The room was getting stuffy, so I excused myself to go splash water on my face, to dispel my distemper. When I returned, the man who treasured houses above cars stood with an arm around Homer's waist and was stroking Homer's hair as they chatted with a third party. However innocently clubby it must have been, I was too drunk on Homer's longtime indulgence of me, now too sexually *spoiled,* I guess, to abide it sportingly.

"Come on, baby, time to go," I said to Homer evenly, like he was my police detective partner, and put my hand on his shoulder. He fixed me with a resentful look only lovers can detect.

"I'll call you this week about the project," he joked to whoever it was. "I have to get Blue back to his cave and hose him down."

Once we were safely back on the ugly, dark street, where I suffered less by context, I sighed, hugged him, and said, "What a relief! Not to have all those rich, beautiful men around you!" He didn't answer.

"It's just a joke," I heard myself offer feebly.

"It was business, Blue. The man's as harmless as a . . . lemming!" He was angry enough to have to grasp at his words, but then he was silent, like when he was recalling old grudges.

"Don't you like that I love to possess you?"

"Don't you ever give me orders in public, do you understand?" he said, pacing at a serious clip.

"Look, I'm sorry, I'm not like that, I guess I've gotten so used
to you asking for orders, that I—"

"Bed is bed. This is real life," he countered. I had seen him get
snappish with his assistant, but he'd never used a sharp tone with
me before. "You know, the collar on your suit jacket was sticking
up all evening and you didn't even notice it."

I instantly felt at the back of my neck and flipped the collar
down, smoothing the lapels for tardy extra credit. "Well, but it's all
the way behind me! Why didn't you tell me?"

"I shouldn't have to tell you, Blue. You should know how to
groom yourself." I must have looked dazed, because he softened
then, and took my arm. "Oh, Hans Christian. I hate to see you suf-
fer like a dumb animal." He turned my collar back up. "There,
that's more *you* anyway."

"Thanks. I am sorry if I seemed jealous."

"No, baby, you stand by your testosterone." He patted my back,
resuming the role he'd briefly dropped. The customer is always
treated as if he's right. We walked in silence for a while.

"I'm trying," I finally blurted.

"I know you are!"

"Remember, I mentioned going to Ohio next weekend, for
Judy's wedding? I know it's short notice, but they just impulsively
decided to do it. I'd really like you to meet my family." At that
moment I thought this was a non-caveman gesture on my part,
but I guess meeting the family is another kind of bondage.

"Blue, of course! I want to meet them! . . . It turns out, I have
to go to Crawford's wedding. It's important, for work. Work disguised as fun."

"Crawford? I had assumed he was gay."

"Well, I guess she's one lonely *principessa*." I didn't even know
they still allowed *principessas*. "He's a trophy, it's rich women's lib.
Think of the gnarlodon financier she'd end up with otherwise."

You rarely see trophy husbands. I always thought it was because women prize real value over looks. Or is it money over looks? You tell me.

"But will they, you know, have sex?"

He winked. "He'll just have to close his eyes and think of the Bank of England."

"I hope you don't think I love you for your money."

"Oh ho! Guilty conscience?"

"No, no. In fact, I wish you didn't have so much."

He gave me a curious look. "What a thing to wish."

Homer asked me not to beat off during the four days I'd be gone, so our reunion would be all the more charged. It was a deal we often made during brief separations, and it was easy enough to control myself when I was a family houseguest. And luckily, there's nothing sexual about weddings.

The wedding was at the sprawling genuine manor of Judy's new security-system-installer husband, Bob, who, like his name, looked the same from all angles, and even in his tuxedo, his football-player solidity did resemble a secure fortress or payroll safe. I had never seen love celebrated while being in love myself, and though I wished my trophy forbidden lover could have been there, I felt a new understanding for the ritual, and felt a part of the story, not an outsider.

Mom was slowing down. It's a shock when you first see age roost on a loved one's shoulders. But she was cautiously happy that her officially lovely daughter was having a big wedding with a band. Ellen's had been modest, those were modest days, and Bridge-out and Kitty were enlightened sixties chicks who had had tiny private ceremonies with acoustic guitars.

Everyone thrilled to Red's newly stellar appearance. He came alone, too, and spread good cheer like a regular guy happily sharing Aladdin's lamp. Judy, of course, was the only contestant at this pageant, and she came down the runway assured of victory. Megan provided the recessional music—"Blue Skies" on the harp is azure indeed—and we all glowed with mutual pride and an open bar.

The reception was a picnic, only with silverware and crystal. I sat with dateless, dark Megan, who teaches rich kids music at Stable and Greenish, outside Boston. Megan's from the quiet stretch of middle kids. She had always kept her silence, the tactful, blank face you maintain on a crowded bus until you can make better connections.

"How are the young masters?" I asked.

"Younger every year, I'm afraid. I had them sing 'Love Is the Answer' for our Spring Thing."

"Thanks for the nickel, Sis! If you can't be nepotistic with family, who can you, blah blah blah."

Megan watched Judy circulate among the white-linened tables, the monarch touring the critical ward. "Isn't Judy radiant? I love her anyway." She'd always been obscured by Judy's glare, but unlike Bridge-out getting angry or Lulu getting drunk, she'd worked, slowly, silently, Mom-like, and made a steady way for herself. "And how are you, Blooper? Anyone in your life? A special person?" She wasn't citing a specific gender, which I took as her signal my Catholic sin was declassified in her book.

"Well, there is." I took the plunge. "It's a wonderful little Texan, named Homer, of all things."

She laughed at the name. "Homer! That's good. I'm glad for you. I can read about Red in the papers, but I never know what you're up to." Megan had dated fitfully in high school, but we never heard about any love life after that.

"Megan . . . Are you gay, too, by any chance?"

She laughed and then sighed. "No, Blue, just tired. By the way, did you know that Judy's pregnant? That's why this all happened so fast."

"Wow. Does Mom know?"

"I think she does, but she may not want people to know she does."

When I got back to New York on Sunday night, Homer wasn't there. He'd removed his suits from my apartment, and he hadn't left a note.

I phoned him to no answer, even his machine was out, so I took a walk and tried him from a sequence of pay phones. I walked all the way to Wall Street. It was warm but late, and I decided to get on a subway to head back home.

At the pay phone on the subway platform, a squat Hispanic man in a parka that made him look like an Eskimo was putting his case to someone on the other end.

"Last night . . ." he said, very slowly, excruciatingly slowly to me, since I was trapped, waiting to use the phone. "Last night . . . you called me an asshole. . . . Why?"

I heard only silence, and then he repeated, "But why? . . . *Why* did you call me an asshole?"

There was another pause. "That is not a reason," he said into the phone finally. "Please. . . . Why? . . . But *why?* . . . *Why* . . . did you call me an asshole?"

This went on for some time, and finally the train arrived. The woman sitting opposite me was reading a fashion magazine that inanely declared, BEAUTY IS BACK!—as if ugliness had been given a chance—and underneath, more startlingly, CAN YOU HOLD ON TO YOUR MAN? You'll never see a men's magazine with the headline CAN YOU HOLD ON TO YOUR WOMAN? Holding on is not a top male priority.

I waited until I got home to try Homer again. I reached him after midnight. He spoke in a monotone as flat as a Body Snatcher's snatchee's, and he pointedly did not apologize. "Look, I forgot about our get-together, Crawford's reception was so stupefying it sort of erased my mental blackboard. I just took my suits to be dry cleaned. You're being paranoid, and it's very unlovable." I was on probation for being stood up. "Look, let's talk tomorrow night. I have a breakfast meeting, and I'm exhausted, and . . . never mind."

I panicked. Besides my confusion, I hadn't ejaculated in five days, and that clouded my composure. "You asked me to save myself up for you. I'm all pressurized."

"Look, I forgot I asked you to. Is that what this is all about? Your orgasm?"

"No, I don't understand what's wrong. What's going on?"

"Blue, I'm feeling corraled. You're pressuring me!"

"This is just bad communication. Let's get together, we can work it out."

He paused. "Okay. Friday?"

"That's a week away!"

"Don't pressure me."

"But I need you!"

"Don't beg! Weakness is not sexy!"

"But this isn't sex, this is real life! Look, I love you, no matter what your health status, I'll love you either way!" I foolishly thought it would help to remind him of my selflessness.

"Blue, you're starting to scare me."

Suddenly my Steady was Unsteady. The Emperor's Nightingale was breaking down. Elvis had left the building.

It was a long week, becalmed at sea. Friday night I took a taxi down to see him—I was too edgy to bicycle—and about halfway there, the foreign driver announced, "My meter does not work right. It goes too slow. I should charge you more." He looked at me like I should volunteer to pay more but then added, "But I no charge you more."

I stared out the window at the passing warehouses, weary in their peeling paint, storage for who knows what. Warehouses, auto supply stores, electrical equipment wholesalers—I was riding down an avenue of adult male reality I didn't even comprehend. After a silence the driver repeated, "I should charge you more. But I no charge you more." I realized he was resentfully forgiving me, like I was doing with Homer, and the tension was not leading to a generous tip.

In Homer's apartment, we talked, but I noticed cigarette butts in his ashtrays, and neither of us smoked. Also, Homer had stopped saying yes and no to things and started answering "That is correct," or "That is incorrect," like a reluctant witness.

Finally he took my hand and spoke with a tender simplicity that was terrifying. "Blue, you're the most real person I've ever known. I've never been so close with anyone else."

Compliments usually precede dismissal. "What did I do wrong?"

"You didn't do anything wrong, Blue. We're getting in way over our heads. Love changes everything, it changes your life. I know, I've been there and you haven't. I don't want to be responsible for your life, I can't make you happy."

Homer, who'd been my plaything, now had all the power. He'd harpooned me and now was complaining that I was dragging around after him. "But you have so far! Last week you loved me. You let me love you."

"I know, but my feelings have changed."

"You said you loved being with me."

"I do, but sex alone isn't everything."

"But why now all of a sudden?"

"I don't know, Blue. . . . You're like a child sometimes. . . . And you're just so strange."

"But everybody's strange. You're strange."

He dropped my hand and punitively looked away from me. "No I'm not. I'm not strange."

"But isn't this a little strange, to say you're not strange?"

"How dare you say that! None of my clients think I'm strange, most of them don't even know I'm gay!" He'd never been angry at me before, and the change was eerie. I Married a Monster from Outer Space. "Don't you see? It's just . . . When I survived that helicopter crash, I was convinced God was saving me for something really big!"

"Well, couldn't that be me?"

He looked at me with a strangled double take, unwilling to insult me or cite my dementia or poverty, but obviously unconvinced I was his station on the love line.

The phone rang, a business call on Friday night, and he took it. Then, without looking at me, he went into his bedroom to make follow-up calls. He was abandoning me in mid-breakup. Was this a test, to lower my boil or provoke it? He had to know I'd be galled, and my struggle not to show it, in order to keep him, made the disjunction more wrenching, like we were grinding between gears while pretending to be on cruise control. I noticed the gifts I'd given him had been put away. When I poked my head into his bedroom, he looked up from the phone angrily and shrugged, like *Can't you even let me finish this business?*

Frustrated at being left alone, I wandered around the apartment. What could account for this change? I looked for some clue besides the inconclusive cigarette butts, and Homer fatefully returned to find me looking through his mail, which was all bills anyway.

"You know, I *dreamed* you ransacked my apartment!"

"Now wait a minute, you can't blame me for what happens in your dreams!"

"I think you should go." His bedroom eyes had become cold. Boardroom eyes.

"But you left me alone in the middle of a very difficult conversation!"

"I had work, it's something adults do, I had to set things up!"

"Couldn't you at least have told me that first, not just disappeared?"

"You're a man, you shouldn't need reassurance."

"But we were having a pretty fraught moment there."

He was silent at that. I approached him, and he let me hug him, as a gesture to brake the runaway train. We both breathed in silence for a minute.

I tried to steer my destiny away from the cliff. "We just have crossed high-tension wires here. Let's go out to the Pines again, do the ocean."

He sighed. "Okay, okay. I can't tomorrow. Sunday night, but I have to throw a party first. You go out to the house, and I'll join you after dinner."

He allowed me to undress and hold him but lay as motionless as a kidnapped bride. Slowly he was turning from satin to stone. In the morning, he wordlessly handed me my underwear, giving a censorious glance at the slight rouge of shit on it. Happier couples might find it earthy and comical, but here I was guilty of a related charge of inelegance. The Brown Badge of Human.

Saturday night I dreamed I had a rendezvous with Homer in a room with track-lit, elegant fixtures and a big picture window. I realized it was a department store window, and we were the mannequins. I had high hopes of reconciling with him, but we weren't supposed to move, and to my horror I realized my nose was dripping, and I couldn't stop it. Then I realized I was farting helplessly, and my stomach was gurgling, and Homer eyed me with tactfully concealed horror. My body was damning me. No matter what I did to reach the castle of happiness, I was trapped inside my corporeal trailer home.

Sunday afternoon, I didn't take the glorious seaplane to the Pines but the more pedestrian, or anyway earthbound, train and ferry. When I showed up at the beach house, no one was there but Crawford, who tried to cover his surprise at seeing me. "Hello!" he shouted heartily. I think he'd forgotten my name.

"Homer's joining me later," I explained. "Congratulations on your marriage!"

"Yes, of course." He smiled faintly, the viscount bantering with the desk clerk. "In fact I'm joining my wife for dinner at her house, so I hope you'll be able to entertain yourself?"

"Oh. Sure!"

I sat on the porch and watched the sun set and the beach crowd dwindle. I was restless but didn't want to miss Homer if he arrived early. At midnight he still hadn't shown up, and I felt convinced calling him would constitute pressure.

Crawford came back alone around one and was surprised all over again to see me.

"Hm. Hasn't arrived, has he?" he said, in an almost human tone. "Well, Homer is a very complicated person, I must say. Very private."

Homer never came. By noon the next day I figured even sane people were allowed to find out What Gave, and I reached him at his office.

"I couldn't make it," he said in a drained tone.

"You couldn't even call?"

There was a silence. I could hear the air moving on the other end, and I saw the dry-cleaned curtains I'd peed on billowing in the bathroom. Finally Homer said, "I did it so you'd hate me."

"I don't want to hate you. I want to understand you."

"Blue, I don't even understand myself."

"But this is a relationship. We're supposed to relate!"

"Lower your voice, I'm at work."

"But what is wrong? What did I do wrong?"

"That again! You did nothing wrong!"

"Am I just, unsuitable?"

"Oh, now, unfair! If anything, it's the reverse! It's me, all right? I have a lot of problems!"

"But you can share them with me!"

"No, I can't. I can't share them with anybody. I have to go, I'll call you later."

I had lopsided dreams of trying to track Homer down in gilded, complicated museum hallways, occasionally glimpsing Crawford hanging paintings which resolutely eluded my sight when I tried to look at them. In one dream Homer was supposed to rendezvous with me at the museum cafeteria, but I found myself seated with and staring at a large, yellow-toothed cretin in burlap, a Bosch model, maybe, who grinned at me as if he were my date and my destiny.

Homer didn't phone, and I sensed phoning him would be interpreted as rape. I did pause outside his apartment building one evening, not, I thought, hoping to run into him—he would hate that—but hoping by osmosis to pick up some data about what had happened. *If I just study the crime scene . . .* Of course he came to his window at one point, and our eyes met, and he retreated hoping I'd think he hadn't seen me. Instead of "On the Street Where You Live" sentimental, somehow it was scary stalker gothic. Not classy. I guess I was afraid of him at that point, which made him afraid of me. You think you control someone when you're ravishing him, but he's the host admitting you: *You may enter.*

Still, he hadn't officially broken up with me. As a mixture of mad hope and stern justice, I was going to insist he spell things out for me. I sent him a dozen roses with a note quoting his observation in the Pines, "We're only on Earth for a few days— You gotta have flowers." After another week I phoned him to see if he'd received them. Homer said he hadn't gotten any flowers, but he had received the note. He impassively joked, "I would have written back, but I was afraid I'd misspell words and use bad grammar. I'm not smart like you." He didn't say anything more.

"Well, what do you think?"

He seemed pained at this official obligation. "I don't want to hurt you, but I have thought, and I do not think we belong together. You want me too much. It's scary."

"But it's called love. If I were indifferent to you, or didn't want the relationship, would you want it then?"

I heard him squirm. "Well, when you put it that way, you make it sound fucked up."

I didn't want to insult him. "But you said I'd make a good father! I mean, you mentioned a house!"

"I'm a complex person, Blue. Let's leave it at that. I have to go, I have an incoming overseas call." I didn't know enough about phone technology to know if that was an unlikely improvisation or testimony to his state-of-the-art gadgets. Well, the brain's a gadget, ultimately. In any case, I thought of the poor cowboy in "Red River Valley"—*Do not hasten to bid me adieu*. Here was Homer hastening like hell to bid me adieu.

III

THE ODYSSEY

11 : GREETINGS FROM
LAKE STUPID

I think of a story Sean brought home from CYO camp, about an Indian brave so in love with a maiden from the tribe across the lake he tries to swim over to her and drowns. The punchline is, *And from that day to this, it has been known as Lake Stupid*. I found myself foundering deep in Lake Stupid, laid low after my unexpected heights, from stand-up comedy to lie-down tragedy.

I was burning up on my awkward re-entry into Earth's atmosphere, tailspinning, Destination Dirt. I couldn't eat, and when a Monahan can't eat, Nature has run foul. I lost fifteen pounds, so I reluctantly recommend the Heartbreak Diet for those who've had no success losing weight through Utter Bliss. Happiness is a tad sedentary, I guess. It dawned on me I was broke, aging, and insane, a shit-stained vagrant who looks like that guy on *Here's How!* I noticed I could see my scalp through my once enviable blond mop: my homeland was facing drought. It seems devilish of God to add a spin to middle age by giving men, in the first nervous flush of decay, literal shining clown heads—adding physical insult to psychic injury. What was that Burma-Shave ad we used to pass on our way to the beach? *In this vale / of toil and sin, / Your head goes bald, / But not your chin.* I was too young to appreciate it. No, wait, rewrite, make that *In this world, / Alas, alack, / Your head goes bald, / But not your back.*

It was all both harmless and unbearable. I was living in the world's dullest nightmare. I don't know if I had a nervous breakdown or not. When I was a kid, one of our neighbors was reported to have had a nervous breakdown, and my mother sniffed and said, "She's just trying to get out of the housework." But I guess I was a little on the insane side. I'd sit watching them rescue a little girl from a well on the TV news, and all I could think was, *Fine, but what about me?* When a comedienne on cable quipped, "I'd love to recapture my youth, but he got himself an unlisted number!" I understood how psychotics think the network newscaster is sending them personally coded messages. One quiz show spooked me when they announced the categories the questions would be drawn from—the Old West, Sex Clinic, Famous Disasters, Bits and Pieces, Outer Space.

And, for instance, I resorted to reading Homer's horoscope in the newspaper to see what he was up to. Lots of financial opportunities and romantic prospects, vaguely alluded to. I analyzed my Chinese cookie fortunes for advice from the gods—"You will lead to a happy life"—Was that a misprint, or did it mean I'd get near to it but never have it, or what?

On a walk I saw a T-shirt for sale that read, "If you love something, let it go. If it comes back to you, it's yours. If it doesn't, hunt it down and kill it." It made me shudder. Was all love fated to end in viciousness? You can tell how ugly and petty the world's sentiments really are by the jokes it makes on its greeting cards. They're all about age, sex, shit, and money.

I despised the romantic songs on the radio, especially the ones about how "I'm Gonna Make You Love Me." Like you could force anyone! Even those old folk songs Kitty dotes on may sound simple and faithful, but "Black Is the Color of My True Love's Eyes" is just as pretend and look-at-me phony as "Monster Mash." And torch songs? "I'll Never Smile Again"? Whoa, there's a plan!

And New York may be a great city to be in love in, full of thrilling spires, adorable shops and byways, and other loving couples—but it's a terrible place to be heartbroken. Everything becomes venal and inane and dross on a colossal scale, a filthy, infinitely large shysters' bazaar full of others, irritatingly, in couples. And here I was, a badly painted church-basement porcelain clown, waiting for the ball peen hammer of destiny to dub me IRREGULAR and smash me definitively from merely junky to junk. People get shot, lovers leap, life seemed too dangerous for me. The city streets seemed suddenly full of sirens, and even the shouts of the children playing in the schoolyard outside my window sounded crass and emotionless. They kept singing a song that sounded like

> *They sang sang sang*
> *till the mainspring sprang*
> *and they sank to the bottom of the sea!*

It's one of those vocal limbo dances where you descend the scale and can barely croak out that last note, and I was sure it was God as *auteur* foreshadowing my own scuttle. And, a final tag, my bed somehow became infested with fleas—not exactly the sleeping partners I'd hoped for. At that point I even considered suicide, but I just couldn't get anything organized.

I lost control. I told everyone about my grief, including sales-clerks and strangers on the bus: *"How am I? Heartbroken." "Sorry I stepped on your foot, I'm dazed and heartbroken."* I may get writer's block, but I never get talker's block. The diarrhea of despair. Amazingly, most people were, or acted, sympathetic. One taxi driver, an African, muttered, "Woo-mans . . . very diffy-cult!" and began weeping himself over a woman in his native village who had married a landowner. Another one philosophized, "Life is a traffic jam of crosses to bear."

My innocuous-seeming neighbor Alice, who looks like she's about to make sandwiches for the menfolk, surprisingly revealed she'd once received a court order not to go near an ex-boyfriend she had threatened with murder. Once we'd traded horror stories, she saw me as a partner in crime and asked me several times to phone a local bar to find out if a man she had a crush on was hanging out there, so she could go and seemingly just run into him. "If a woman phones, they'll know it's me, but you can just pretend to be one of his dumb friends." It was all in itself depressing, but it reminded me that lovesickness is epidemic. Communion! Yes! Too bad it's in pain.

Lloyd, however, warned me one night, "Boo Hoo, even your best friends don't want to hear your problems more than three times." When I bewailed Homer's elusiveness as that of a frightened child, he snorted, I guess because it was the third time. "Frightened child? How about shifty phony? How about reckless drive-by dating? I fucked a lot of liars, but at least I never went out with one."

"But he said he loved me."

"Well, he would say that, wouldn't he?" Lloyd emitted.

"Oh, you would say, 'Well, he would say that, wouldn't he,' wouldn't you?" I tried to counter. See, Lloyd mistrusted ambitious men and always spoke warmly of his unemployed, poky friends in San Francisco who survived by house-sitting. "Get out of New York, Blue, it's a haunted house that possesses all its tenants!" Despite his manic edges, Lloyd did understand one Californian virtue. "They go to San Francisco to enjoy life, but they come to New York to be *successes*! You can't settle down on a treadmill."

"But he seemed better than that."

"Poor Boo Hoo, his slave left him! And look at you, you've got your health! *You're in fucking good health, you should be ecstatic!* But no, you're addicted to pathos, tears are your alcohol. Well, alcohol is your alcohol, but you just love your self-portrait of suffering. Come on, Boo Hoo! Sing 'Danny Boy' now!"

"I'd just never had anyone need me before."

"You're like some deluded vestigial heterosexual! You want your partner younger, smaller, and submissive! You're like some straight bully ogling the wee secretaries at happy hour! You want *devotion,* Brandon de Wilde in *Shane,* you want *Heidi,* and not even the female version of that exists! Women may be built to receive, but that doesn't keep them from planning conquests. Nobody's that simple. Everybody's angling for control."

"That's not fair, Lloyd, I just want to be valued."

"What you just want is someone with a bigger inferiority complex than you. The semiconfident fuck the unconfident. A sissy who'll mistake you for a man."

Why do the desires of the penis sound so criminal when factually described? The business of the penis, zoology will back me up, is invasion and explosion. But like I said, I wanted to think of it as Communion.

Red was more forbearing, the older brother on the phone. "Well, Hanker, every spill is a chance to clean the floor!" When I responded that I'd slipped on the spill and couldn't get up, he went on. "It isn't just your love that didn't pan out, bro'. I'm amazed that any relationship ever works even briefly, not that they collapse."

"I wonder if it was because I didn't have money."

"I doubt it. If you loved this guy he must be better than that." Red, my other eyes—we trusted each other's sense of treasure— never got to meet Homer, which made him even more illusory in retrospect. "But it's true you aren't *secure.* No offense, but he probably realized you're a little on the insane side."

"But everyone's insane. That's where love comes in, neutralizing others' insanity."

"Yeah, maybe, but it's a fact a lot of people don't want to deal with. And maybe you weren't his *kind* of insane."

It was demoralizing, though, to realize, from a distance, that Red was having difficulties, too, just much more expensive ones. It was weird to get his version and the media's of his tempestuous relationship, as the magazines termed it, with, for starters, a tennis starlet famous for racket-hurling tantrums and togs that kept coming off on the court. No one ever says no to beauties, so they develop telekinetic destructive powers. She slammed a car door on his hand, and her name became synonymous with Mean for stand-up comics, even though Red said it was an accident. Then there was a three-times-married soap actress whom other women disliked—"Always the bride and never the bridesmaid," one TV gossip simpered. And then, a supposed supermodel named Suede—"Don't blame her," Red emphasized. "Her hippie parents actually called her that." And it all seemed even weirder for being distorted and hysterically shouted at me by those We-Stalk-the-Stalker strangers on TV. For one thing, it was stretching the truth to refer to Suede as a supermodel. One drug arrest does not make you a supermodel. I urged Red to settle down, since I wanted to, but he moaned, "Brother, I can't even commit to watching one TV program. I sit there flicking the remote control. Men are promiscuous even as couch potatoes."

Red was also notorious for betting huge sums on football games, basketball games, even his own Emmy chances, and there was a story in *The Midnight World* about him dropping a bundle in Vegas. And, lucky for him, he merely nearly drowned when his cord broke at a celebrity bungee jump at Lake Tahoe. The Sinatra gene in his classiness chromosome was mutating dangerously. Failure and success are both hard to handle.

I myself had to jump to avoid the trapdoor of poverty, so I got a frustrating job playing background piano down at Que Sera Sera, where well-dressed obese men would offer me a twenty to stop while they made phone calls. I also did society parties, for a flat fee. A very flat fee. "*Drape* the place in Gershwin," one hostess told me. Music as decor, that's what I was reduced to. Also, I was terrified I'd run into Homer, or else maybe that's why I took the jobs. And, inevitably, one night I did. It was like eating cinder pie.

He was the tuxedoed foreman at the private room of the Central Park boathouse, which was being decorated with flags for some political thank-you dance. I had arrived early to see if the piano was in tune enough for guests to ignore. He had just been joking with an assistant.

"There's an idea! Designer flags!" He laughed. "Not red, white, and blue—but rose, bone, and periwinkle!" The second he saw me, however, the champagne drained from his face.

"Homer!"

"Blue." His voice was reluctant, as if he'd run into his mom while leading his gang to a rumble. "I didn't know they hired you, I'm sorry. I asked Devon's assistant to get a college kid." My fee was low enough to confuse me with a student.

"Well . . . I am working my way through the school of hard knocks!" It was like trying to tickle your tax auditor. "Um . . . How are you?"

"That's kind of personal."

"You look well."

"Stop that."

"Well, I miss you."

"It's the past you miss. Accept it, Blue."

It was like a twenty-second limit on an overseas call. "Are you seeing anyone?"

He rolled his eyes in exasperation. "That's none of your business." Someone hanging bunting waved at him. "I have to go."

He receded into the red, white, and blue yonder, and a chattering curtain of desperate lobbyists, both political and personal, came between us for the evening.

12 : THE LOST WEEKNIGHT

My birthday, I mean, our birthday—Red and I were losing touch—came around. Beggars' Night again. I invited Lloyd to come over and mitigate my agony, but he didn't return my message. I phoned home for a swig of There's Always Mom tonic, but she sounded exhausted, and for the first time ever was in a hurry to get off the phone. That worried me.

I knew somewhere they'd rent a restaurant to throw Homer a party, and I had only the fleas for company. The night was chilly, and I was having one tall, cold glass of lonely. Actually, I was having tall, cold juice glasses of the champagne that Red had had sent—a whole case, but no note, just a generic happy birthday tag. Drinking's a lousy stopgap measure—alcohol's such an Indian giver. It's borrowed happiness, borrowed at a destructively high interest rate. I will say this for Dr. Bushmills, though, he does make house calls. It's a vacation in a can, the poor man's Riviera. Except, the return trip is always on foot.

And unfortunately, that night the Waters of Forgetfulness were tainted with facts, and I drank the Mud of Remorse, I felt the creeping shame and panic I remembered from childhood. My riled Irish woes. *Lord, I am not worthy that you should come under my roof. No one must see me, I must hide.* I AM SORRY.

Then some religious nuts came to my door with a spiel about the reunion of body and soul at the last judgment. "Are you nuts?" I found myself yelling. "What kind of religion tells you to avoid the temptations of the flesh and then saddles you with flesh for all eternity as a supposed reward? Isn't the idea to *graduate* from appetite? You're just pagans! You have to see yourself and your god in the form of actual animal bodies! No thanks! I'm shooting for Nirvana, folks! Nothingness or nothing!" I slammed the door.

I heard a cat in heat yowling outside my window all night that seemed to cry "I! I!" over and over. Us animals, beached in our bones. It was driving me crazy, and at that point it wasn't a long drive. I leaned out the window and yowled, too, at the moon, and its wordless, simultaneous promises and denials. It pulled tears out of me like a tide.

Finally I fell into that wretched sleep of the fully dressed and dreamed I was packing to go somewhere, though of course I didn't know where. I was in the dark attic in the house in Cleveland, but all the objects I was packing were strange to me—a small toy carousel, a locked jewelry box, an old illuminated manuscript—and I didn't know if I needed them or not, not to mention whether they were even mine.

Then, suddenly, I was visiting a rich man's house I guess I had been packing for a weekend. The whole dream started evaporating the second I woke up, but I guess the host must have been Cuddles, because he was huge and humorless, like a drill sergeant. Anyway, they were playing some kind of You're Dead tag with guns that actually hurt when they fired at you, around a huge swimming pool and its labyrinthine overhanging catwalks. Someone got shot and fell dead into the pool, to my surprise. I defended myself saying, "I don't know the rules! It's my birthday!" But I still had to run around, and, worse, I didn't know anyone else, so it's not like I was among friends. The gunfire somehow tore and stained our clothes, but Cuddles kept providing free replacement clothes. I remember running in fear past one of the guest bedrooms and seeing some nice new pastel clothes folded on the bedside table. Maybe we were actually being injured and repaired, like the warriors in Viking heaven, that most hellish of heavens. Then I was in a kind of gift shop, like the mansion suddenly turned into a museum, with gift books, little art objects, and even big tubs of free ice cream, courtesy of Cuddles, I guess, including a strange pink-and-blue marbleized color. "We're still trying to perfect that flavor," said Dana, my old college roommate, who was standing with me in waiter's whites. "It confuses people. Is it for boys, or for girls?" And I wondered, What, does he work here? Couldn't the Kennedys land him a better job? There was Homer, briefly, but he was busy back in the museum gift-shop office, making deals, I guess, and couldn't see me. As always, he disappeared from sight. I tried but couldn't figure out what this display or museum shop was all about. There were lots of calling cards in a crystal bowl—from lawyers, designers, even a blacksmith (for wealthy people's wrought-iron design needs?). I was frustrated with myself for having no money and not even comprehending who everyone else was, or what the bowl of cards was for—to win a free dinner or join a secret society? I didn't know whatever these people knew. When I woke up it was Lloyd phoning to wish me happy Halloween morning.

13 : DEAR ANXIOUS

Later that day I ran into Kip Lastly—the little honey-colored guy who'd played Telemachus in *Odyssey!*—by the remaindered bin at Music Forever, and he suggested I go to an Alcoholics Anonymous meeting with him. Kip had had a hard time, being small and cute and straight in the musical theater world, always having to play weakling roles, resist gay men's advances, and find women tiny enough to date. His was the opposite of Milla's problem—she had a hard time finding men tall enough. They say it's an age-conscious society, but it's just as height-conscious. The tallest presidential candidate always wins, right?

Anyway, ever since student council I've dreaded meetings—at least at the theater the crowd sees a *plot*—but after my birthday bender I thought I should investigate all avenues in Fog City. I know, San Francisco is Fog City, but once when Lloyd was wearing his Fog City sweatshirt someone asked him where Fog City was, and he said, "Everywhere, baby, everywhere." Another time a tourist asked him how to get to Bleecker Street, and he answered in his cruelly kind style, "It's right between Bleak and Bleakest."

I got really nervous before joining Kip, and in my distraction downed a stiff Absolut. Hey, no one needed me, and at least I did manage to resist drugs. I don't know if Kip could tell when we rendezvoused—I'd read that the stars of Hollywood's golden era drank vodka on the set so their Personal Hells would pass undetected on their breaths—but he was friendly at least, and not critical company like Lloyd.

I don't remember the meeting very clearly, except that everyone was smoking in the hallway and gulping coffee inside. One woman tearfully announced she had shoplifted some towels she didn't need, and I sort of dozed through another talking about her insomnia. The people seemed supportive and all, and Kip literally bucked me up several times. Afterwards, I chatted with that discontented twin I told you about, the one who didn't even speak to his brother. He'd been to two other AA meetings already that day, so he'd replaced one addiction with another.

All right, I was drunk at an AA meeting, that moment was the absolute, or Absolut, bottom, but at least now I knew I wasn't the only one having trouble with life as an extremely difficult Required Course with Involuntarily Perfect Attendance. But I needed friends who were already in the lifeboat. As we filed out of the church basement, I noticed on the bulletin board that this was All Souls' Day.

Kip gripped me in parting. "Monahan, you may be bigger than me, but hear me on this or you'll destroy yourself. You have to take responsibility."

I was terrified of going to daily meetings—it would've been too much like school—but I didn't want to just disappear like my dad's brothers, so I resolved to draw on my reservoir of *unspoiled.* I embarked on a daredevil one-man plot to save me from myself.

I made an appointment for a physical and crammed for the exam by teetotaling and working out for a month. I started bicycling around Central Park every morning and found it too was a quick poor-man's vacation, and no quashed feeling after.

I also went to visit my college roommate Dana at his upstate commune, where there is no drinking or vice besides underground comic books and what looked to me during their worship like foot fetishism. Dana was surprised that I'd visit but seemed to like fresh company, and I never told him I was using his temple for my rehab center. Their daily Remind Me I'm Convinced meetings reminded me of the fundamentalist service I'd been taken to the summer I counseled at music camp in Indiana, where the minister put his hands on me and asked me if I'd seen the light to want to be born again (under his showman's baton), like it was a stage trick requiring audience participation, but I'd smilingly resisted. He'd concealed his frustration by gently, if loudly, sending me back to my seat with a Fare Well, Brother. I thank Mom for that implacable resolve, at least in that setting, and in this one, where Dana was determined to get me to bow to the mousy woman who'd been deeded the divinity of the late Perfect Master. Dana seemed fine, in a sluggish way, like a teenager in Shangri-la, but I knew he'd wither and die if he ever left the property. I guess it was his clinic, too. He'd spent his life in private schools, so maybe he was seeking an extension of that version of home.

When I finally did see my doctor, he declared me in perfect health, though he didn't realize I had pulled an all-nighter to get it.

"I yam feeling purty damn doomy, Doc," I told him, a sleek, sophisticated Arab who shaved his head and wore impeccable suits instead of a smock. I talked to him in a funny voice to make measuring my mortality less frightening. "I'm heartbroken. What do you prescribe?"

His lips pursed as I imagine Omar Khayyám's might have. "Time," he answered.

"But I'm so edgy! Is it me, or this city?"

Coolly, he recited, *"And in this palace of illusions, ever restless men pursue phantoms."* I was too scared to ask if that was Moslem wisdom, or what. "Try to get out of town," he added flatly.

If only I could have, but Fog City's everywhere, baby. The advice columnists are always saying, "Dear Anxious, Get Help," but it's expensive, and I had to look high and, mostly, low to find bar-

gain counsel. Don't ever choose a therapist from a personal ad in
The Village Free Paper. It said "Sliding Scale," that was the clincher
for me.

Naughton LeBlanc wasn't actually a psychiatrist, or even a li-
censed therapist, but he *virtually* was, he said, in his soothing voice,
and he only charged me ten dollars a visit. Imitation Help. However, it's like budget brain surgery—you'd better wait for the
brand name.

During our sessions, he played New Age music, which was
supposed to be relaxing, but it meant that instead of saying, "How
do you feel about that?" he usually said, "Could you repeat that?"
He insisted my older brothers must have sexually abused me and
regularly urged me to describe what that must have been like. He
told me the way to get over Homer was to describe sex with him
out loud until I got tired of it. I started to feel like the old porno
storyteller, and when he kept criticizing me for resisting letting
him massage me, I expressed my doubts.

He expressed his disappointment. "I think your friend may be
right about you being straight. Your genetic double is straight, you
like smooth-faced partners. . . . And you obviously take no interest in clothes or grooming."

"Lloyd was *kidding.*"

"I wonder if mere kidding is really possible. Quick—who are
you angriest at, your father, your mother, or yourself?"

"Well, are you eligible as a write-in candidate?"

That was pretty much that. I told him I didn't have any more
money for therapy, which was true enough. When he offered to
start paying me, I knew I'd better leave. I started simply talking out
loud to myself, at home, and on the street, to much better results.

Seeking another new way up and out, I asked myself, "What do
divorcees and ex-cons do to survive?" I figured I was along their
lines. And the answer was: *Take a class.* So, I joined a night-school

songwriting class at a place called the Learning Basement. The stark classroom's contrastingly Viennese teacher, Fritz Middling, was born a bit late for the operetta style of his music—you'd recognize his "Sandman's Waltz" from *The Ragamuffins' Holiday*— and a bit soon to relate to the thirtyish students who'd resorted to his instruction. I was edgy from the very first class, when Middling had us listen to "Night and Day" fifteen times in a row. "Please hold your comments until we are finished!" he announced tersely, but the bell rang before we could discuss whatever we were supposed to have learned. Still, I'd already paid my money.

Herr Middling thought Gilbert and Sullivan a bit too outrageous, but he blandly tolerated the atonal meanderings his students unspooled, nervous intros to melodies that never arrived. The most cheering aspect of the undertaking was that it made me feel relatively sane and glamorous. I wasn't inspired, though, and couldn't help writing bitter parodies that made everyone uneasy, like "Ungettable, That's What You Are" and "My Really, Really, Really Foolish Heart." At my bilious low ebb, I tried my hand at pure unwholesomeness, to kill my inner student council president. I wore sunglasses while I played it, to lend me an icier style. It went something like, well, exactly like, this:

I'm just a typical consumer
Stores are my schools.
In the halls of Mazuma
I know Spondula rules.
There's them as got
and them as not
are fools.

I want a stack of jack, Mack—
Just lemme hack at that snack pack.
Just a dash of cash, Flash,
and I can crash some smash bash.

I said a sled of bread, Fred,
and watch me shake that bedstead!
Oh Jimmy Jimmy Jimmy!
Oh gimme gimme gimme!
Big eyes, big hands, big me.

I want a show of dough, Joe.
I'll have a go at à go-go.
With a batch of scratch, Satch,
I could catch some snatch, natch!
I would look keen in green, Gene—
I'd bean a lean teen screen queen.
Oh do me do me do me!
Your limousine's so roomy!
Big car, big star, big me!

It's better to be driven.
Give and you're forgiven.
I'll pay you and you'll fake it!
Unwrap it and I'll take it!
It's easier to touch than to feel!
I want sacks and sacks—
Let's face the facts.
You can only fuck what's real.

"I don't believe that Anglo-Saxonism at the end is a proper word for songs," Middling offered after a parched pause.

"It's supposed to shock," I explained.

"*Snatch* and *fuck* are not shocking. They are disappointing."

Well, that depends, doesn't it?

The final test of recovery is to handle new misfortune. I loaned my apartment to Lloyd for a Christmas party, since Lloyd lived in what he called an inefficiency apartment, "a broom closet where the broom couldn't fall over completely." Lloyd's announced theme was A Victorian Christmas, and he borrowed several dolls in period dress from the window dressing supply of the department store where he worked—I could never imagine him speaking to customers—and positioned them diorama-style in my living room as smudged children in a workhouse, or dying of diphtheria, or being slashed by Jack the Ripper. The Victorian-style Christmas tree in the bedroom, which Lloyd insisted on, blazed with real candles, but the presents underneath it somehow caught fire while the guests—all strangers to me, mostly Earthlings—were just arriving, and it destroyed most of the apartment and all the clothes Homer had given me. If God was making a point there, He could have just sent a note. Weirdly, the dolls all survived unharmed. I will say, however, that there's nothing like a disaster to take your mind off heartbreak.

My hands and arms got burned trying to put out the yuletide fire, but it didn't seem to bother me. The fire was impersonal bad luck; it had none of love's confusing aftereffects. However, after two days in the hospital, I discovered I no longer had insurance coverage. Believe me, the Insurance Company That Cares exists only in the TV commercial. First, they said I wasn't covered at that time, then that I had never been covered by them. The burns weren't bad, but being told you don't exist is unsettling. Milla's brother Upo had gotten me a deal with his jewelry makers' and home craftsmen's guild, and the insurance company had evidently smelled a scam. When they challenged my affiliation, I emphasized that I did craft my songs at home. Institutions have no interest in metaphor.

I figured I was ruined, or whatever the modern word for it is, but when I checked out of the hospital, I was told my bill was already paid. Lloyd, who hadn't visited the hospital, had phoned Red, who'd taken care of it. The nurse handed me a message she'd taken down over the phone. It was her unfamiliar handwriting but Red's voice: "Thanks for the college education. I'm sorry I haven't used it."

14 : A DARK NIGHT OF THE SOUL
ON THE TOWN

There's an old joke about a comic who's hired to entertain at a senior citizens' home, and when he comes out and asks the crowd how they're doing, they answer as one, *"Cough cough. A little better, thanks."* I took my daily dosage of Time, just as my doctor prescribed, and slowly I recovered. Now I could face facts. I just couldn't stand them.

One day I was watching this science-fiction movie on TV, waiting for the seasons to change, and the space victim was being lowered into boiling lava, and I said to myself, "Well, I'm heartbroken, but I'm not being lowered into boiling lava." That's when I knew I was going to make it.

Then, about an hour later, there was a nature film on public television about animal courtship rituals, and that helped, too. Man, those animals are as crazy as we are! People are always admiring animals, and, boy, there's a lot of misplaced faith. Males killing each other, mice dying after sex, spiders eating their spouses, salmon climbing waterfalls only to be eaten by bears, cuckoos giving away their kids. Even without songwriters, they somehow messed themselves up! God's plan is a practical joke!

Then there was a breaking story about a washed-up pop star who'd just murdered his ex-wife, her mother, and then himself. It made me feel better about myself. Wow, I behaved badly with Homer, but I didn't kill him! And I drank too much, but I didn't kill myself! Blue! Nice work! That resolved me to ride out my in-born difficulties. I had looked for the answer from God, when I should have just concentrated more closely on tabloid television.

Also, I guess I had some ad exec about my age to thank, but my childhood hit resurfaced as a detergent jingle—"Dirt is the question, Pow is the answer!" If you're on TV you are valid, and solvency does solve things—I was less ashamed, I was current. Days went by when I didn't think of Homer—he'd become the occasional thicket, just an off-and-on obsession. I started to get out of the apartment more, as if my broken heart had had its cast removed. It was like the animals in *Bambi* leaving their tree trunks after the winter. Since the gang I'd hung out with in my twenties had dispersed to Los Angeles, marriage, or Purgatory, I was a wist-fully lone wolf.

Lloyd had felt guilty about destroying my apartment and ac-tually made an effort to be friendly as well as accessible. He called me one night and said, "Hey, you melancholy would-be Dane, I just got paid for playing First Corpse in that TV movie, so I'm dead but flush! Let's go play Love Lotto! Come with me to the Wet Spot." He meant the Deep End, a swimming-pool-themed disco, and I welcomed his company, though he could be peevish even when we were supposedly having fun.

I'd certainly wrung my fun from gay bars, and I met Homer in one, but most of the time they're Unhappy Hunting Grounds, strictly shutter safaris, dark, noisy stores full of Grade A inedible eggs, and the aimlessly agitating music appropriately sounds like the unavailing repetition when the needle sticks on the record, though, astonishingly, people mouth the words, all three or four of them, over and over, like demon monks at vespers. The Deep End was typical, though its poolside pastels and simulated shimmering water lights added a touch of the Californian ethereal to the Satanic Mill darkness. When we arrived, a few pain-eyed guys in clothes happier than themselves were standing at the bar, drinking, smoking, and chewing gum all at the same time—three-ring nervousness. Dancing shadows from the video monitors played on their faces like free-ranging tattoos, though otherwise they stood or leaned immobile—disheartened refugees, camouflaged in a dim detention center. There were posters for an upcoming Mardi Gras costume contest with a top prize for MOST TRAGIC, and I marveled at the unintentional lack of irony of it all.

Some disco-style incantation was playing, a single lyric repeated over and over:

Things change.
Things change.
Things change.
Things change.
Things change.
Things change.

Since the song itself didn't, I wondered aloud, "Does that mean that things do change, or that they don't?"

"If you're analyzing disco lyrics," Lloyd said, "I further suggest trying to decipher wallpaper patterns for messages from aliens." He lifted his drink like he was making a chess move, narrowed his eyes, and appraised the scene, as always, the foreign correspondent.

"If you lost twenty pounds you'd be really sexy," one plastered youth paused before Lloyd and observed. Lloyd had let himself go since his *Odyssey!* days.

"And if you gained twenty IQ points you'd still be an idiot," he snapped. As his dashed suitor retreated, he muttered, "Anyway, I won't be overweight for long."

"What do you mean?" I asked.

He looked blank for a second, like a computer screen summoning up a program, and swiftly answered, "I'm resuming my old stringent regimen, the old weight lifting and water. After tonight's imbroglio, of course." He sipped his drink in summary, perfect dramatic timing. Fragments of light from a spinning mirrored disco ball overhead swarmed over him and me like an unfelt plague of locusts.

There was a woman next to us, clutching an Evian bottle for grounding, dazed and smiling as her male friend chattered. I caught myself thinking, One of the *nice* humans is here! Did that mean I like women, or patronize them, or just sympathize with hopeful souls in strange settings? "Stop feeling for her!" Lloyd barked when he saw where I was looking. "Give her credit. She's as bad as anyone else."

He entertained himself most of the time, even when others were trying to, and that night he kept improvising new lyrics to the songs playing on the sound system. When the old Barry Manilow song "Copacabana" came on, Lloyd feigned disco fever and sang as he danced, heaving his fists aloft like a repeatedly victorious boxer:

> *Music and dancing*
> *and husbands from Lansing!*
> *Boozers and losers*
> *and out-of-it Hoosiers!*
> *At the Copa*
> *I fell down drunk!*

Lloyd didn't understand that I *wanted* someone Out of It, since being In It seemed to make people tense and heartless. As a songwriter, though, I envied his ability to make things up on the spot, which was his specialty in that unpaid *Earthling Hour* in which he shone. He never did the same sketch twice, and he never slept with the same man twice—a life of variety and high speed. His was a genius no one has ever been paid for, and his triumphs evaporated in a second, so his talents frustrated him, like a brilliant jet pilot who can't get a job in the eighteenth century. I used to sit in awe and watch him improvise musical versions of *Gone with the Wind* set on Mars, or a sea chantey about a dental student in Ancient Rome in love with a dog, all from shouted audience suggestions. So he was doubly irritated by the drag performer here, the self-dubbed Lady Remington, who was stuffing dollars in her borrowed cleavage, an abundantly talentless lip-syncher presuming to host the evening, commandeering it, really, like a terrorist or a mean drunk on the subway. "Soliciting applause for a song Barbra Streisand sang thirty years ago," grumbled Lloyd, who was used to making up operas onstage. "He doesn't even have an act! I may be desperate for applause, too, but at least I have an act! Illusion is one thing, delusion is another."

Her prepared remarks were hostile and trite, and when the crowd didn't cheer wildly enough, she berated them for not getting the jokes. Then she paraded up and down the bar, a slow-moving tantrum, and Lloyd murmured, "Aren't there leash laws?" When she sought a dollar from him, Lloyd shouted, "I'll mail my tip to Barbra. She did the singing!"

What mystified me was the sexless shelf this rude Lady chose to retreat to, a glittery secret hiding place, a loud limbo. Weirdly, like the nature films I'd watched of the puff adders and horned gemsboks, and complex insect mating dances, it reminded me again that animals are mired in ritual. However, this guy made it hard on himself, or should I say his selves, in all the categories men and women usually do. Seeking and failing to conquer or be conquered in one insincere torch song.

The place got busier, pushy and tense, more like rush hour than a party. It was too crowded to meet anyone. "Well," I tried to mock the dark fracas with pastel words. "If the birds don't alight on our fingers, we can still watch them fly through the sky."

Lloyd hated poetic excuses for selfishness. "Except your finger isn't the appendage you want them to land on, is it, Saint Francis?" Up on the video monitors they were showing home videos of Fire Island parties, naked men dancing on the beach, to go with the bar's aquatic theme. One muscled body can be erotic or neurotic, depending on your viewpoint, but hundreds of them wriggling in close confinement is horrific, like a live bait bucket. And there—*Show me no more, Spirit!*—was Homer, laughing, dancing, walking, slyly grinning. I didn't know any of the people with him. The screens, several yards overhead, were emblems of some cabal, of distant happiness in an unreachable dimension.

"Terror in the Year Five Thousand!" Lloyd boomed, like an old movie trailer. "Where love is forgotten and a heartless nudist society prizes only beauty!"

"That sounds a little like right-wing hysteria," I murmured guiltily.

"No no," said Lloyd. "No wings. I'm wingless."

Suddenly, Alden, the lawyer from Fire Island who had always tended to look past me for his real friends, appeared, unusually jolly to see me. I got it: he wanted to meet big, burly Lloyd. Phizz was with him. It was an odd reunion of the cast of my Homer Days. Phizz was without dog but held a teddy bear he'd just gotten as part of a tote bag of goodies at an awards banquet.

I was about to introduce them when Alden quickly said, "Hi! Alden Powers," and offered his hand to Lloyd like an animatronic president. "Would you like to dance?" he asked Lloyd before learning his name.

"I would," Lloyd responded. "But in this world, how can you?"

Alden laughed and started to tell me about his latest purchases, so it would be less obviously to impress Lloyd. Lloyd had no use for this keeping-two-cars-in-an-expensive-garage-is-a-bitch offhand pretension, but he nodded at Alden's run-on monolog like he was overacting the nice guy in a skit, a bored peahen watching the peacock display his tail.

"Who is this guy mistaking himself for?" he whispered at one moment, and instantly resumed nodding at Alden. "Yes, the bankruptcy laws do need overhauling."

"It's not often you meet a Californian who's smart!" Alden grinned.

Lloyd smiled winningly, which I knew always prefigured a scene. "And it's not often you meet a New Yorker who's stupid," he cooed. Alden looked as if he had awoken suddenly at the wrong board meeting and, cutting his market losses, just walked away. As I said, Lloyd mistrusted ambitious men. "I should have pointed out that Robert Frost was a Californian," he reflected.

"I guess you and Homer broke up?" Phizz asked, now that he had to talk.

"Well, I certainly did," I answered, which clearly irritated Lloyd, who turned away to face the din.

"Well, Blue, I liked you, anyway!" Phizz offered by way of re-assurance. "You were a nice break from those big studs he went through for a while. Ooh! I know how you can meet new guys. Just go to every thousand-dollar-a-plate fund-raiser you're invited to. That way you meet only the A-list men." He kissed his teddy bear as the talisman of his tale. "That's how I met Derek!"

"How is Derek?"

"He's in Abu Dhabi, if you can believe there is such a place."

"And . . . uh . . . how is Homer?" I asked, more anxiously than I wished to.

"Oh, his company's flourishing! He's so much more lovable than Antonio, he lured away most of his customers! He moved, too, to a huge new place. *Hee-yuge.* Oh, and he went on an im-pulse trip to Europe! Just picked up and went! He's hosting Eu-ropeans all the time now and dating this very powerful German man who's like the governor of Berlin. They trade weekends, it's jet-setty! Look, I better go find Alden. Your friend was kind of mean to him, you know."

The swift mention of my successor caught me off-guard, and I shivered as Phizz moved on. I shivered again when I saw my doc-tor, the elegant, shaven-headed Arab, across the room, wearing only a leather harness and codpiece. You never get used to seeing your doctor naked. Lloyd returned his gaze to me, seeing that the coast was clear. He growled at the room.

"And the worst part of it," he said of the newly absent company, "is that those guys are happy and we're not."

An older man, not so old really, about sixty, but in a gay bar it's striking, ambled past, friendless and stoical. "That's me in ten years," I said.

"Oh, don't be silly," Lloyd said sweetly. "That's you right now." Lloyd never tolerated self-pity in others. Then he wandered away, too, which he often did, he would never say where. "Don't follow me," he called without turning his head. He never came back.

I noticed a strange man staring at me, drawn and pale and blue-skinned in the darkness, like Marley's ghost, only the chains on his leather jacket were subtler. Finally the specter approached me. "You used to go out with Homer Winger, didn't you?" he asked

"Yes." I hesitated. "Yes, we went out. Unfortunately, it was a round trip. How did you know?"

"I saw you with him a few times. I saw you. I used to date him, too."

He seemed more of a visitation than a date. "Are you Derek?" I'd imagined Derek as more of this Earth.

"No." He smiled bitterly, mistaken for a millionaire. "I'm after and before Derek. Homer goes back to him from time to time. My name doesn't matter." It felt sinister, like I was meeting someone from the Underground, who had to tell me the formula before the poison takes effect. "Anyway, don't blame yourself. That is one very messed up individual. He's an accident waiting to happen to someone else!"

"Well, he did leave me very suddenly, I never understood it."

"He leaves everyone suddenly. That's what he knows. He told me all about it. His mother ran off, his daddy beat him, he kept running away to find the same place he just was. Use and be used. He hitchhiked out and up. What's that bigoted hole he's from?"

"Petty?"

"Right. You can't think much of yourself in a town that hates Mexicans like that."

"I don't understand."

"Homer's mother, whoever she was, was Mexican. Didn't he even tell you that?"

"No." I examined my memory of his face. Yes, I could see it, in his grin, his dark eyes, in his embrace.

"Well, of course not, he looks white enough if you're not in a boondock that's obsessed with considering someone inferior to them. He was taught to hate himself. Add gay on top and you've got Quicksand."

"But aren't Latins white? I'm confused. And anyway, he's free of that here, isn't he?"

He cocked his head doubtfully. "Nothing changes your race, except maybe money. Derek helped. He got on. He's ambitious. But he'll always feel he's a fake in that nice suit, and he has to flee. 'Love me, no, I don't deserve it.' He'll never put Petty behind him."

I realized we were still in the disco, the music was blaring, but I'd forgotten. "Homer told you all this?" I stammered.

My anonymous new intimate seemed to have become preoccupied and looked hurt in a way that contradicted his heartless black leather. "Three months he lived with me, after his deadbeat dad died. That may be why he needed me."

"I thought his father was alive. The scientist?"

He didn't seem to hear me. "He left a note. Three fucking words—I AM SORRY. You don't leave a note, you tell a person to his face." I AM SORRY. I wondered if Homer had had any catechism classes.

"It's all so unnecessary," I said. "He should be proud of himself."

"Tell a few million other people that." He seemed to regret having worked himself up this way and put his empty beer bottle on the bar. "Hey, I know why you're obviously still so hung up on him. He's got the hottest little ass in New York."

This insulting compliment made me shudder, but not for Homer. Was that true? Had I been just sex crazy and not noble? Had I been *dick*tated to? I thought I'd cherished the pearl of great price, and here it was the hottest little ass in New York. And on beyond why I longed for Homer, the question was, Was this story more true than the other one? He may have presented one version to this guy and another version to me, with the real facts lying somewhere between or beyond. Homer certainly had secretive, pained moments. And he tested his charms wherever he went, as if to reassure himself they worked. Maybe he'd compulsively over-sold himself to me, like I was a practice customer, and bolted once I took him up on it. The need to be loved isn't always matched by the ability to love. Well, an explanation for the ghost doesn't stop the haunting, but it's a relief from the Unexplained. I felt freed but not helped. Out of the prison and into the desert!

Homer's hexed ex had left, and Lloyd was AWOL. The sixty-year old who'd passed me earlier settled in beside me. He blinked at me briefly and said, "You and me—we're too old for this!"

I'd been drinking seltzer, but that made me order a Deep End zombie. I could swear it had chlorine in it, but I guess zombies shouldn't complain about the pleasures of the living.

15 : THE SIBLING CIRCUIT

As I expanded my morale-building exercises, I figured a decathlon
of family visits might tone me up. Family is what you discover
when the rest of the world proves hostile and demonic, right?

On the strength of the Pow commercial, I tested my luck in
Los Angeles, insidious land of the Lotus Eaters, trying to write
more jingles or movie themes. I stayed with Red at his pool-free,
ramshackle home in Los Angeles, but he worked extraordinary
hours, and I barely saw him. I met his friends from the show, all
straight, even the skinny actor who played the shy, bookish one. I
never suspected showbiz was so overrun with heterosexuals.

The city itself, if it has a self, gave me a gnawing, hollow feeling, like when you think you're eating food in a dream. At least
New Yorkers' abruptness is the frankness of honest intercourse.
Hollywood—you could cut the superficiality with a knife. People
track-lighting their homes from outside to show them off at night
like the Arc de Triomphe, or no, make that a Denny's, all flashy
and flimsy. *Getta loada my Chattel!* Or as Homer would say, the
Looky! ethic. And all that sunshine—even the weather is shallow.

Anyway, I couldn't even get a job writing songs for a Saturday morning cartoon series. It was to be called *The Love Lizards*—

the creepiness of lizards was supposed to lure the kids in, I guess, and then they covertly hit you with the love stuff—but I don't think it ever aired. I can't blame them for passing on me, because my heart wasn't in it and the samples I wrote for them were on the downbeat side:

> *Sometimes you'll be sad,*
> *the sun will go away.*
> *But don't think you are bad,*
> *Being sad's okay.*

Red had to go to Hawaii to feign fun on a game show, so I decided to go back to New York. Before leaving, though, I had a meeting with my supposed mentor, Sonny LaMatina, who's now a professional guest star, a leathery showbiz senior citizen trying to find a hit. I asked him what he wanted to write next, and he answered, in an adolescent whine that was weird from an old man, "It's not about what I want It's about what they want." He made a sweeping gesture out the window, toward his lush yard.

"You mean—the flowers?" I was recalling his concert for the trees.

"No, I mean . . ." Pot had slowed his speech.

"Oh! Your public!" I guessed.

"No, no, the producers! They're the ones who make it all happen."

Instead of flying back directly, I decided to make a side trip to visit brother Sean in Seattle. Sean had always been the quiet Beatle in the family—brown, boyish but ominously still, with unexpressive, dark brows, one of the forgotten middle kids who tended to slip away at family fracases. He ran cross-country in high school, and we always joked that, after graduation, he decided it was a good idea. Sean does Handicap Awareness for a big aviation corporation. He blindfolds workers or puts them in wheelchairs for a day to make them sensitive to the needs of disabled people when building nuclear bombers. The Monahan men, we want to be macho, yet we want to be good.

I arranged to visit only overnight, since Sean had never worked at conversing with me and I didn't want to take a long ferry ride to face any awkward silences lasting more than twelve hours. Standing in his tangled yard overlooking the gray water, twiddling with the branches of his dogwood tree, he surprised me by softly reciting, "Come see the real flowers in this painful world." I must have looked bemused, because he added, "It's an old haiku." I guess the Pacific rim had put him in touch with Orientalism.

The twilight, and the absurdity of the drizzle dampening both of us, led me to try personal questions, as I never would have at home.

"Are you seeing anyone?"

"No, not now." We headed back into the house.

"But you were?"

"Oh, you know that Sinatra lyric, Blue, about I could tell you a lot, but I've got to be true to my code?"

"Sure." It wouldn't be classy. Sean Bears All In Silence, the noble whiteskin. Through his vast picture window, I saw mist begin to consume the mainland across the water. It was a little clammy in his darkling living room, but Sean sat without turning on a light.

He sighed. "I will say this, Blue. Don't ever let anyone tell you that Asian women are easy to handle!"

I'd timed my itinerary like a political campaign. On the way back to New York, I stopped in Ohio for what ordinarily would have been a non-obligatory party on Ellen's so-called farm, to celebrate George's retirement from Waste Management.

My plane was delayed because someone jokingly mentioned guns at check-in, so it was already evening when I got to Ellen's. It's not really a farm but an old house surrounded by fields, though when we were kids it seemed like a country estate to us. Ellen doesn't grow anything, "except enough squash to annoy people with at harvest time." Across the front porch hung a banner that read, NOW YOU CAN LEAVE WASTE BEHIND YOU.

"How do you like Conal's handiwork?" Ellen gestured to the banner dryly, the indifferent tour guide. "You missed Mom. They just left. Lulu's driving her back to the house. Ever since her overnight in the hospital last month, she has this thing about sleeping in her own bed."

"Lulu took her?" Lulu had been the disgruntled one, squashed near the bottom and overshadowed by Judy above and the Grand Finale twins below. Where the older girls were fine-boned and tall, she was small and got Dad's tough Bowery Boy jaw. Instead of complaining out loud, she'd become a temporary secretary and full-time wild girl, in fatal fidelity to her nickname. She cooled her boiling waters with sangria, and at thirty-five had suddenly been hit with a moral hangover.

"She and Mom are getting along now?" Littler Lulu used to tear up books to get Mom's attention. It maddens librarians.

"When Mom got sick, Loony moved out of that Singles Camp right back home to take care of her. She's done a complete turnaround. Mom's sickness has been her salvation!" Ellen announced even good news grimly. "And it's made her know she's useful. She's on a roll, she's met a guy, finally, one without a probation officer attached! A race car driver. Not exactly a banker, but not a biker either."

The fact that Mom was ill gave a sober undertone to what otherwise seemed like the boilerplate family frolic. Nobody took a swing at anyone. Free-range grandchildren flitted past, noisier than their size and abrupt in their turnings as the fireflies they chased through the damp, comfortingly funky grass. I noticed Red had sent a case of excellent champagne, at this point practically his signature gesture of Regrets. Kitty the booster, down from Toronto, always eager to be impressed, conceded she was wowed. "I'll be forgettin' meself!" she imitated Mom's counsel against putting on airs, and a bit of champagne was indeed helping her forget herself. Conal joshed, "He should stay away more often!" Conal's once-carrot hair and Howdy Doody freckles and ears had obliged him to be zany or be ridiculed, the live wire of his Illuminating Company maintenance team. But George groused, "Why did Red have to send a *girl* drink?"

The children flowed past again, and, following their trajectory, I was shocked at the sight of a dazed-looking old man in a wheelchair. "Ellen, wh–who's that?" I stammered, strangely frightened.

"That's John, Dad's brother, didn't you see him earlier? The wino. Sorry, sobriety-impaired individual. They found him in a homeless shelter in Columbus. Some other geezer recognized him. I'm surprised the Creature hadn't killed him ages ago." It took me a second to remember the Creature is whiskey.

"My God! How did he live, all those years?"

"I don't know. I guess he played Santa Claus. Don't expect patter from the guy," she cautioned.

Judy sat with him, an angel mystified by her all too mortal charge, and she made soft, soothing babble he gave no sign of hearing. ". . . I don't know, I just wish Bob would tell me things that bothered him, sometimes," I heard her shyly confess as I neared the bench. At least Uncle John might still have a career as a therapist.

"Hi, Blue!" She smiled. "We're all really excited about Pow!"

"Sisterness—you are so good." I touched her bare shoulder. "Saint Judy the Apostle!"

"Ohh," she demurred, knowing that good girls reject compliments. "I used to want so much to be good." She sighed and gazed at the fireflies as if they had somehow succeeded at it.

"I guess we all did. I used to sit at Mass hoping Father Demchak would announce how good I was."

"Well, you won a few titles."

She grinned at the grass in embarrassment. "That wasn't really being good, though. Did you ever do this? I used to say a dozen complete sets of prayers every night. A dozen Our Fathers, a dozen Hail Marys, a dozen Acts of Contrition, a dozen Glory Bes, and a dozen Apostle's Creeds. Just in case any of you, or Mom, would forget to say your prayers, so you wouldn't have the venial sin on your souls."

This was slightly unnerving, but you have to admit, this was a girl who tried. "No, uh, it never occurred to me," I said finally. "I did use to wonder if I'd go to hell for not loving God, since I couldn't even see Him."

Now it was Judy's turn to fail at a comeback. "You . . . were just a child," she offered in my defense. Inside the house, a toddler was plunking out the first four notes of "Silent Night" on the piano, laboriously, over and over.

I thought I should return to Earth. "I hear you and Bob do your own TV commercials! I hope I get to see one while I'm here."

"I'll give you a sample." She sighed, sounding tired, but adopted a self-mocking singsong. *"Carhart Security Systems knows. Nothing is more important than the safety of your loved ones!"* Across the yard I saw her giant Bob nodding attentively to a monolog on Irish independence from little George.

"Well, you certainly are secure!"

"Well, as secure as anything in this crazy world!" The perfect beauty pageant answer, with a welcome touch of world-weariness. She adjusted slumping Uncle John in his seat as if he were a mannequin, then gently patted his cheek as if to apologize for the intrusion. She sang him a few soft bars of the lullaby Mom had sung to us and presumably she sings to her little Belinda. Judy is more lovable now that the crow's-feet at her eyes have made her less dully stunning and more credibly lovely. I don't know if she touches up her perfect golden hair or not. Monahans don't ask about such things.

She considered John's vacant face, Aphrodite contemplating the bust of Hades. "He doesn't talk, or seem to recognize faces, or move, or anything," she regretfully admitted, as if it were confidential information. "I just . . . I wonder if there's someone in there. Like the way people in comas sometimes hear what's being said."

His taxidermy eyes, free even from despair, didn't indicate any such hope, but the faint rise and fall of his chest, and his trembling fingers, indicated tenancy, at least. His face resembled Dad's photo, or even my face in the mirror, but cruelly aged, of course—cruel aging is redundant, isn't it?—pale and translucent as blood-soaked paper tissue.

"I'd love to ask him about Daddy," continued Judy wistfully. "There aren't any photos, no records, his family didn't keep any of that. It's like, that whole generation has been erased." She stroked John's thin hair, grass in the dunes. "At least ours has video."

I saw Bridge-out sitting alone and got up to join her.

"Blue?" Judy said. "I'm sorry I made you play Living Statue."

I wanted to laugh but answered somberly. "You . . . were just a child."

I sat at the picnic table in the deepening dark with Bridge-out and watched Judy's little Belinda hopelessly heaving a horseshoe a foot or so in imitation of the adults who'd been playing earlier.

"She'll brain herself trying to act grown up!" Bridge-out offered mock sports commentary. She was in the process of divorcing her husband, a successful surgeon Mom had only pretended to be joking about when she said, "A doctor in the family! As Mr. Baum would say, I'm *kvelling*!" Raj Nadir was certainly brilliant, and handsome in an imperious I Am Your Pharaoh way. He marshaled medical minutiae like they were military maneuvers, and the few times I met him he conversed with me like he was tired of trying to get whatever it was through my thick skull.

I sipped some champagne with Bridge-out in silence, but as an amateur of the amorous, I had no wisdom to offer. Judy carried Belinda away from the remotely dangerous horseshoes, and Bridge-out sighed. "He was so dazzling, and Mom had taught us to revere intelligence. Ellen married her principal, for God's sake! But Raj thought he was the general of everyone else's body, including mine. I thought I was strong enough to match him, the spirited lass in the Harlequin romance, but he wanted an old-fashioned Indian wife, the kind you burn when you're tired of her. It was Dysfunction Junction!"

"You're strong, you'll get through this."

She squeezed my hand and got momentarily teary. "You know, telling me I'm strong helps, I need to hear that." She paused and regained control of herself. A firefly lit on her glass and took off again.

She resumed. "I was trying to find another dimension, when what I needed was to fix up the dimension I was in. I built my honeymoon cottage on a volcano. I thought it was funny that Father Healy who married us was Cleveland's leading exorcist. I didn't realize teasing a sacrament was going to backfire on me." Raj had gone on a rampage at his hospital. When a colleague accused him of malpractice, he'd chased him with a scalpel. "At least when that happened I could be a little relieved. I knew it wasn't just *me* causing the trouble with my neediness."

I told her about living through Homer. She didn't bat an eye at the gay angle, which relieved me, though I would have liked somebody in the family to act a little surprised.

"I never even got to argue with him," I concluded. I must have sounded jealous of her battles. "It was just suddenly, silently over."

Bridge-out smiled inscrutably. "Men don't like to argue. They like to kill, but they don't like to argue. Raj always ended things with 'There's no use talking when you're in this state.' So, now we're in separate states."

"Well, as Mom would say, Thank God there are no children involved. Well, except for you and Raj. Have you told Mom?"

She looked uneasily at her fingernails, as if Mom might show up and announce one of her spot checks on them. "I just can't, Blue. She's sick, and I don't want to worry her. Besides, Raj works odd hours. She doesn't suspect anything's wrong."

"Well, I know it's hard to tell her personal stuff. Post No Ills. I still haven't come out to her."

"Oh, she must know, Blue, she just doesn't want to hear it."

"I just hope she isn't, you know, ashamed of me."

"No, no. . . . Well . . . No more than she would be if she had to visualize any of us having sex."

Somebody knocked over a tray on the porch, raising a clatter. "There were no survivors!" Ellen called jokingly. George—who'd replaced Jock in the Alpha Male role, forbidden to be a cop but free to play one—had been gesturing, loudly explaining to Bob some point he had already explained, and accidentally upturned the tray. Ellen always said George put the *deafen* in *definite*. Like Kip Lastly, he had that perpetual short-guy catch-up to do. He went after Dad's record, too, but he only got as far as five daughters, another runner-up's frustration—Jock would have had sons! His once insolent adolescent crew cut was now reactionary, and, of course, it was now white, as if invisible dragons his namesake never knew had scared it. I admired his singing voice, but he'd always been remote to me, out of chronological distance and crowding as much as anything else. I noticed that George was drinking too much and chain-smoked. Hey, all right! This compact pillar of superiority was as compulsive and nervous as me, in his own way. What a rush of love I felt for him. Bridge-out leaned over to me and whispered, "He feels guilty 'cause he's not dead like Dad and Jock. We all feel guilty for being alive. It's that Kick Me, I'm Irish thing."

George and Conal then tried a two-man version of "In the Still of the Night," with neither the designated melodic driver. Ellen shook her head and said, "What a bunch of senile delinquents." She turned to me. "I have something to show you! They've all seen it. Come on inside."

"A mystery! Should I bring the champagne?"

"Sure, we'll have our own little Cannes."

Ellen had been widowed early after marrying a much older man, to escape home, yes, but also to be good and rescue someone else. It was her version of getting shot, I guess. I remember Xenon at their wedding, with white hairs visible in his ears and nostrils, as if his head were full of cobwebs, and even at age seven I sensed that a groom should look fresher than this. Plus, I was scared of the fact he was a high school principal, a teacher's teacher. She seemed self-sufficient, though, and didn't seem to mind living alone after her own son grew up.

"Going through junk, I found some old Super-8 home movie footage," she told me, slipping a videotape into the VCR. "I was a dope. I thought Xenon was rich because he had a home movie camera! Plus his Old World manner, where you act successful even when you're not. And of course he had the Farm." She fussed with finding the right button. "Don't think of me as a gold digger, Blue. It wasn't the property I was after, it was the breathing room. This was one farm that had no animals crowding it up!"

"What are we screening, Film baby!" I imitated the real imitation phony staff at *The Love Lizards*.

"My John had a friend transfer it to video." Clumsy hand-held footage swooped and hiccuped across the TV screen. "Xenon took them that summer he was actually nice. It's somebody's birthday." The Farm's landscape was exactly the same, but the rushing children there clearly didn't guess their middle-aged selves were spying on them. The print had faded; everything was a soundless, underwatery blue. Red is the most fugitive color. There were Jock, George, and Conal playing football with a cantaloupe, or maybe it was a football with the red drained from it.

"Gosh, Jock looks like a little boy there." I stared. "I remember him as so huge and powerful!"

"He was insane, Blue. Walking across Lake Erie!"

"Well, it *was* frozen at the time."

"But at night?"

"The ice was firmest then."

"Still . . . that's reckless like oldest sons aren't allowed to be," Ellen recited, like the unperturbable narrator of wildlife footage. "And that pressure just tightened the straitjacket. He knew he couldn't be good enough to make up for Dad! That car crash was no big surprise."

The screen was idyllic, however. There was then-long-haired Kitty pushing Lulu on the swing that fell down years later, years ago. And then, there was Dead Old Dad.

Still pictures aren't mistakable for life, but movies make you jump, when the dead walk, not to mention make faces. He was shrugging, looking like Red today, only with Jock's bulk, and he was unsure what to do for the camera, so he acted Acting and started demonstrating Tragic Postures—Grief's headache, Fury's double fists, Ecstasy's tiptoe. Hey, that martyr was funny! Then he got really near the camera, making to devour it. Dad had fillings! Xenon must have slipped, because the image jumped to children with food smeared on their faces. Red and I looked so small I confessed I wasn't sure which of us was which. I still catch Red's face in a tailor's three-way mirror, sometimes.

"Well, that's easy," said Ellen, pouring more champagne. "Wait and see which one starts crying." Ellen could be brusque, but I felt safe with her. She was free from sales pitch.

"That film is a great find!" I toasted her. "It's weird, I feel like I love Dad so much, and I barely remember him. I do recall him wearing the dish towel like a babushka and singing 'Molly Malone' like the pathos in it was really funny."

"He was great when he was actually around. That must be where Red gets his enchanted idiot routine," Ellen observed.

"Dad really should never have been a cop, he was a lousy cop! He was Ferdinand the Bull, Mom even bossed him around. Dad was the thirteenth child. But it was the Depression, there were no options. Cleveland didn't have sitcoms, at least nothing public you could get paid for."

To me as the youngest, these were tales of lost Atlantis, and I listened as minimalist Ellen uncharacteristically held forth. "And Mom, thirty years later she probably would have been attorney general. If there was a Nobel Prize for home economics, she would have won it." On the video, Mom was shooing the camera away. She considered it a foolish luxury. "She had her strange compulsions, though, just like anybody who's fit for high office. You're the lastborn, you missed most of the movie, Blue. Yes, she was good at pinching the pennies, but having us count our milk money out five times over, like the coins would change number in our hands like a magic trick? Having us bring the garbage back in, not once but twice, to make double sure nothing useful had been accidentally thrown out?"

I remembered being frightened once in kindergarten, Mom had buttoned my winter coat, and paused to count the number of buttons on it, over and over. I didn't think it was odd, I assumed adults knew what they were doing, I just didn't want to be laughed at for arriving late. Now, there I was on the video, crying.

"And those 'retired and damaged' books from the library?" Ellen went on. "I think those were courtesy of *klep-to-ma-nia*." She parodied the last word like she was fresh from Freud's office.

"Oh, how could she have stolen books?"

"Who's going to find out? She was the librarian. She could remove the cards from the file. Mrs. Dumbock was so out of it even I once walked out with two books in plain view just to see if I could do it, and she was smiling away in her lavender lilac land."

"Ellen! What a risk!"

"I knew that's what would happen, though. And please! I returned the books." She poured some more champagne for herself and me. Wow, I was palling around with a senior officer! On the TV, Mom was displaying a bowl of potato salad that could feed a chain gang.

"I think I understand it, though," she continued. "You knew Mom's parents died in the flu epidemic, and you've seen photos of Aunt Agnes, you know her idea of self-indulgence was a pillow to kneel on when you said your nightly rosary."

"Sure, Mom always told us how lucky we were."

"She also had a sister who committed suicide as a teenager, did you know that?"

"No! Are you sure? How did you find out?"

"Old Hunkajunk let it slip, she thought we knew." Mrs. Hankojanek had lived across the street. Her outdoor Christmas nativity scene always featured a prominent BEWARE OF DOG sign.

"Between Agnes and the isolation, Eleanor opted for Door Number Three. And the nuns she and Mom had at Immaculate Body must have been the olden-day maniacs we luckily missed. Once when I complained to Mom about having to wash the kitchen floor, she told me a nun had made her wash an entire gymnasium floor with a shoelace and a teacup of water. She had to keep emptying and refilling the teacup. It was supposed to be a parable told in torture, I guess."

Life was a precarious business, Mom had deduced, and her orchard of children and accomplishments was to shore up against mortal night, or at least give it a run for its money. God had taken her parents and sister, Dad and Jock and the miscarriages. He at least owed her a few crummy books. Birds must build nests.

"And here we sit with champagne and videos." I could only be hackneyed at such intensity.

"Yes, don't you feel guilty?"

"Well, not enough, I guess. Ashamed is more like it."

"Oh, why, Blue? Because you're *different*?" She said it like she was tweaking sensitivity in general. Apparently this whole crowd had smelled the coffee.

"It's like *Fiddler on the Roof*," she went on, increasingly blurry. We weren't exactly hammered on champagne, but it was tap, tap, tapping at both of us. I didn't understand her allusion, except I remembered she'd soloed on violin in her high school's all-Christian production of it. Then she elaborated. "We older kids were very disciplined, very orthodox. I respected authority so much I married it! Then the younger ones got crazier and crazier—Bridge-out and Raj, Sean and his Japanese girl. Red! And you're the caboose of the circus train! The cherry on the parfait."

"Well, the *imparfait*."

"Oh, don't be so fancy. You always had to be different! Red was smug, but you're narcissistic." She looked at me with Mom's famous cocked head of caution: *Don't be spoiled.*

"I didn't want to be different, though, I wanted to belong. And anyhow, I turned out to be just like everyone always told me I was."

"Well, no one ever put it in so many words. Everyone gets teased when they're small. Nicknames are just a mean way of saying I Love You. Jock called me Smellin'. Guess what, I lived and bathed. Do you think Bridge-out liked being told she was nuts? She didn't actually go nuts, then. Well, bad example. Anyway, we didn't mean to make you blue. Hey, there's an old song title for you."

Ellen's John, my alarmingly graying nephew who's taller than I, leaned in through the screen door holding his sleeping toddler. Brrr my sister the grandmother.

"Are you all right, most esteemed drunken parent?"

She smiled sourly but clearly enjoyed loverlike teasing from him. "Well, I'm listed in good condition, oh adorable excruciating extraction of my womb."

"They're getting ready to take Great-uncle John back to the slammer." He meant the nursing home. His voice even in jest was like Ellen's deadly monotone, and he never raised his dawn-of-man brow. Jock all over again. But he's a fireman, not a cop. All the danger but none of the killing.

We steadied ourselves and headed back outside, where most of the family had returned from the field and were packing up children and lawn darts for the trip back to the city. Megan was playing her laptop harp, and George was singing the folk song about the Devil bringing the henpecked man's wife back from hell because she made the place too unpleasant. Bob listened politely, like a candidate for office, and George's wife tolerated it because it was George's night. "That's lovely, Megan," she said.

"Isn't it wonderful the way we all get together?" crew-cut Kitty gushed. She gushed, but she stayed up in Toronto for years at a time with her period-piece hippie husband, her viola da gamba, and her Early Music Ensemble.

Judy wheeled Uncle John toward her car, and, as fragile as he looked, he seemed to brighten when the wheelchair bumped going over a tree root.

"There goes all my loose change!" he cackled feebly.

Judy gasped and started to cry, which didn't go with her strawberry blondness and floral sundress.

"The old coot!" Ellen murmured admiringly. "Laying low on the Lord, I guess."

I slept in Ellen's guest room that night, and all night long an owl repeated, *Who? Who? Who? Who?*

Not much of a melody, but you can't beat those lyrics.

16 : MY DOUBLE'S MATE

I was finally fully paroled from my country-western-style purgatory by country music itself. I wrote a purgative song that Randy
Battles heard on a demo tape (thanks, at last, to my Sonny LaMarina
connection) and recorded.

> *Although it's quite a blow that I've been dealt,*
> *I've felt a lot of things I'd never felt.*
> *I now know what it feels like to be dirt,*
> *so thank you from the bottom of my hurt.*
>
> *I'll never fall again the way I did.*
> *I'll never slide as far down as I slid*
> *From now on I'm on permanent alert*
> *to tell a faithful lover from a flirt,*
> *so thank you from the bottom of my hurt.*

And so forth. You know Randy Battles. He always wears a
white cowboy hat but otherwise dresses all in black. I think the
image is "I'm the good guy, but I'm sexually dangerous." With
that twang of his he reminded me of Homer, and that broad Texan

jaw looked like his ancestors must have conquered the West by chewing it up. When he sang "I'd Walk a Thousand Miles for You," women acted like he already had. The funny thing about pop stars like Randy is, they always sing about devotion and being turned down, but it's hard to imagine that they're devoted or that anyone's ever actually turned them down.

So, the song made money—I'd sued life for heartbreak and it settled out of court. I was happy just to be healthy, though success gives you that freedom to be. Lloyd, I presumed in a jealous pique because of my hit song, had stopped returning my calls, so I looked for other social options. I simulated dating, though nothing that counted. Exhibition baseball, really. On a flight from Nashville I met Reed Vogel, a polished-penny bright flight attendant who made perky his policy, most impressively because he was HIV positive. By the time he told me that, I liked him well enough to keep seeing him, and I was impressed by his Mennonite-stock courage, especially since it was disguised as silliness. I dreaded going down that trail of tears with him, though, and for the first time I could see why Homer might have run from even a healthy man when my need, that universal illness, became apparent.

I felt I should bring it up. "You're being very good to me when you know I don't intend to get serious," I told Reed one evening at his apartment full of Hummel figures and maddeningly pert all-night cuckoo clocks. We dated without sex—comfortable potatoes, no meat.

"Well, catering to crabby people on the red-eye has made me appreciate even temporary kindness."

"You don't mind being my temp, my, I don't know, my courtesy car?"

"You're being honest. I trust you. Besides, even if you were serious, I'd probably be dead before you could prove it."

"Yike."

"I didn't mean to scare you, Blooey. I just have to demonstrate that trying to be cheerful doesn't mean I'm in denial."

As nice as he was, I secretly wished he didn't call me Blooey. It made me feel like an explosion in a comic book. His baby talk did imply he wasn't seeing reality straight on but with miniaturizing glasses, for safety. Still, he'd achieved something, what Dana was searching for up on his Philosophy Farm. "Yes, I panic sometimes, but *thank God* my union has good insurance! And of course the first thing they teach you is how to keep your panic from your passengers, and you're like a nice passenger on a flight of unknown duration."

One telephonic night Red announced, "Guess what! I'm getting married!" and then added, "On the show!" Grogan was supposed to be a middle-aged mama's boy and a slob, and it was theorized to be doubly hilarious to see him wear a tuxedo and wed his long suffering girlfriend in the final episode. The bookworm was to make up with his stuffy father, and the former athlete was to be inducted into the fictional wing of the Football Hall of Fame. Case closed, pending reunion specials.

Red reported uneasily on the sensation of rehearsing even make-believe marriage. "Wearing a tuxedo was no big deal, Blue, I wear those to roasts, whereas Lylah"—the actress playing the bride—"kept squeaking about how strange it was to wear a wedding gown, how she'd collected bride dolls of the world as a kid, and, even though she wears leather pants off camera I think she does want to marry that ever touring rock drummer of hers. The real trouble is, the real weird part is, I've started seeing Jeannie Howe, the casting woman, and she's been constantly making satiric references to the big day, and reminding me that she cast my bride."

The episode was a smash, the way death boosts a singer's sales, though the show instantly headed into syndication. "It's as if my shadow were earning money for me while I slept!" secretly hardworking Red exulted. "Isn't it great? I never have to act again, unless I want to! I'm between a pillow and a soft place!"

He certainly had more time for the phone now. "And Jeannie? I'd just looked past her for years. She already liked me, I trusted her, and meanwhile, I was trying to decode Mystery Women! She really aces all her events, Blue. In order of their appearance, she's sexy, smart, good, and, rarest of all, she's willing to take me on! I got all four cherries lined up on the slot machine! Jackpot!"

My good fortune made me able to exult in his, too, though I worried that Red was completed, all love and money like the last episode of a comedy, and I was left adrift like an unending soap opera. Still, you have to take comfort in any proximate stability.

Jeannie came back to New York to cast a movie, and, at Red's suggestion, we met for lunch, at Que Sera Sera, where I'd played cocktail piano years before. I arrived first and was greeted by the manager, who introduced me to my current equivalent, depressingly, a former concert soloist. I was relieved I had graduated from the joint, anyway, and sat down with that freed feeling of just visiting a former workplace. When Jeannie saw me and headed for the table, I was seized by a powerful good feeling about her. She was both dishy and decent, like the spouse who comes running to you on a life insurance commercial, and she softly ridiculed the meeting she'd just had with the film's producers, who'd spent two hours reaching the agreement that the finished work should be *good*.

I was gradually unnerved and aroused, though, by the realization that her fair skin, brown eyes, brown hair, and good-humored Texan drawl were eerily like Homer's. She had his attentive gaze and wry, secretive smile, too, as if her very thoughts were entertaining her while she concentrated on you. I almost asked her to stand up again so I could compare her height with his.

"So, you're in town to cast a movie?" I asked what I already knew.

She rolled her eyes in self-deprecation like Homer would. "I'm just breaking into features, so I can't be too choosy at first. It's called *No Crime Like the Present,* and it's pretty criminal itself. Nothing but hookers and Kaboom. Your Randy Battles is up for a role."

We ordered lunch and chatted about old movie trivia, about who'd almost gotten what classic part except for makeup poisoning, and so on, though Jeannie pointed out, "The old stars were great, but I have to concentrate on living actors. I can't hire the dead."

At one point she laughed without enjoying it, and said, "Forgive me, it's just strange to see someone who looks so much like Robert and yet isn't." I guess she called him Robert to distinguish herself from a mere Hi Red pal.

"I don't mean to spook you, though I must say you look like someone I know, too!"

"I mean, I can see the differences. In casting, you look for subtle differences in emotional qualities, like colors or, well, for you in music, halftones on the scale. I'll see a dozen tall, blond men for a part, I have to tell them all apart."

"Well, Red and I have been weather-beaten in different ways."

"Your eyes are different, too. Like if you had been kidnapped and raised by a different tribe." I heard that. Life may be a river, but more exactly it's a river delta, and every branch you choose or are swept into changes your course. Some jostling in the womb, a few minutes between births, a few playroom power struggles, and we who were one were already on different tributaries.

As the lunch progressed, Jeannie playfully referred to Red as TV's Affable Barfly, the phrase *TV Guide* had used to profile him. She claimed generally to distrust actors but thought of TV's Barfly as "a harmonica player with a hobby," and, shrewdly, she took me into her confidence, so she and I would have a bond of our own. "He's a wonderful, funny, smart man. But I worry about his gambling," she said. "It's no big deal, but it's like his overeating, he's making up for hungry times, I think. There *is* a tomorrow. I want to teach him to *relax*." Red only played a lazy bum on television.

"We're both gobblers," I offered.

"Well, on the up side of that, you both clearly have a passion for living." She could see how to cast an actor as either villain or hero, as need be.

"And lunch. I apologize for eating so quickly."

Before we could begin to wonder which of us would pay, the waiter revealed in a luxurious hush that the lunch was complimentary, for a distinguished former employee. It's strange—once you have money, they give you a free meal.

Jeannie gathered her purse, and we walked into the bright, frank sunlight.

"I'm glad you don't find it weird dating a guy with a body double."

"Well." She squinted and smiled, just as frankly. "I remember my mom telling me when I started dating, 'Just watch how he treats his family, 'cause that's how he'll treat you.' So if you two have a good relationship, that can only be a good sign for me. Oh, I admit I get jealous when he gets you on the phone and starts chattering at high speed like you were computers trading programs, but it's a good sign of how crazy about life you both are."

Whoa. A healthy prognosis from a relative stranger is one of life's greatest tonics.

17 : MELTING

Reed's company was sweet, but I needed some woof as well as tweet in my music, and continued to try to reach Lloyd. He wouldn't answer my phone calls, and, as I said, I assumed he was punishing me, or himself somehow, for my success with the Randy Battles song. Lloyd took offense easily, so it could have been some inadvertent flub on my part, or he just got tired of the moony, heartsick phase I'd been in. I got concerned when his phone was disconnected, though.

I knew he wasn't doing *The Earthling Hour* show anymore. One of the members told me he'd announced he didn't like whatever it was they were going to make up from then on and just quit. At the store they said he'd notified them that material objects do not verifiably exist, and, therefore, he couldn't in good conscience sell them to people. I went to his landlord. It turns out Lloyd had moved out, and no one knew where.

Finally, Milla phoned me. Women do the tough phone calls, the emotional chores. She'd gone to the hospital to see a friend with AIDS, a chorus boy encountering old age decades ahead of time, and she'd seen Lloyd there. He'd kept his illness a secret from everyone, out of pride or shame, you tell me.

I found out his room number and brought him a pile of Classic Comics Illustrated, *David Copperfield, Of Human Bondage, Vanity Fair.* I figured he'd relish the lame but colorful reduction of great ideas to revue sketches. He lay in a tangle of sweaty sheets, staring at the ceiling, this usual electric storm of energy, and, as with Mom, it was frightening to see what had roosted on him. "Lloyd! I had a hard time finding you!"

He took a moment to see who it was but then didn't look at me. "Well . . . Lately I've had a hard time finding myself." He could see how shaken I was by how gaunt he looked. "Yes, darling, I have managed to lose some weight," he used a society matron's lockjaw. "I'm aiming to get down to a size zero."

I felt that futile mix of urgency and aimlessness you get with the dying. My Classic Comics seemed an ill-chosen joke now. Ritually, I had to ask, "Can I get you anything?"

"No, thanks . . . ," he murmured, and continued to look away, as if distracted in a large store. ". . . I'm just browsing."

I tried frankness now. "Why didn't you tell me, Lloyd?"

He hated the idea of another earnest conversation with Boo Hoo. "Because . . . I could just imagine what your pity would be like. All sweet and useless, like a sponge bath in maple syrup. And really, you'd be gloating. *'I've survived!'* This makes your Homer trouble seem silly, doesn't it? The sight of me does you good, doesn't it?"

Being ungallant was Lloyd's code of honor. He felt it was his duty to spread unhappiness, like the fox in the fable who's lost his tail. Except Lloyd was losing everything, bit by bit, an unwilling Cheshire cat who wasn't grinning about it. He noticed his sheets were arranged so he appeared to be sinking into them, and he pretended to be the Wicked Witch after Dorothy throws the water on her: *"I'm mellll-ting! Melting!"*

His volume made a brisk, nice-nanny-type volunteer appear, and she asked Lloyd if there were anything she could do for him.

"Yes," he snapped. "Lie down on this bed and assume my illness for me, and I'll go annoy the rest of the patients for you." Lloyd spoke to others the way most people do in their cars, to other drivers, who can't hear them.

"I wish I could," she answered without offense.

"You do not. Say *I can't*. That at least isn't hypocritical."

"Your friend has a very sharp mind!" she observed to me and exited. "Enjoy your visit, lads!" I was her transitory foothold to escape from rock slides on Mount Lloyd.

"She is trying to do good," I pointed out, though goodness was unimpressive to Lloyd.

"Oh, I must write her a note, then," he cracked. "Thanks for coming by to wave as I drown!" He yelled that out to her, but the effort made him gasp unexpectedly, and he fell back like a man shot. After a long minute he started talking again, though I'm not sure it was to me. "*Do good*. . . . People say, save the Earth. But really, why? Most sitcoms last what, five, six years? How long has that thing your brother's on been wearing out its welcome? Movies last what, two hours? You don't say, I wish this movie were fifty hours long! Life is three billion years old. Enough is enough. It's the same story again and again. It hurts to be greedy, but you die. We get the joke already."

"But Lloyd—I don't get it."

"That's why you're going to live, Blue, and I'm going to die. It's your punishment for ignorance."

Several self-consciously bouncy guys from *The Earthling Hour* arrived with old movie magazines for Lloyd to read, including one whose headline read, HEARTTHROB'S HOSPITAL HORROR! Lloyd was weakening, so all he could do was mime screaming to add to the joke, or else he was enacting his fury at everyone finding out about his weakness. Then Lloyd's father appeared, uneasy and at a loss for words, fresh, if one can be, from Silicon Valley in California. This was the man who showed his support for Lloyd by mailing him clippings about gay serial killers with BE CAREFUL scrawled in the margins. After a clumsy silence, he finally grasped at a straw and asked if anyone knew how the Dodgers did that day. Of Lloyd's four male visitors, no one did. One of them, though, to keep the ball rolling, asked where the Dodgers were from. After a pause, another asked what sport they played.

"Oh God," Lloyd moaned, only it sounded like he was addressing someone, not swearing. Then his breathing got labored, as if the room were clogged with smoke. "Somebody press Fast Forward."

Life has no Fast Forward button, and no Rewind. Only Play. And Stop. Lloyd canceled his own show a week later.

The night after he died, I had trouble falling asleep. Crying usually brings the benefit of exhaustion, but my half-closed eyes kept presenting the spectacle of what looked like amoebas skittering across my wet, hazy corneas, like the restless wraiths on a microscope slide. *I'm not a man, I'm the mountain where the amoebas farm.* I drifted off and dreamed Lloyd was ringing my doorbell, and of course I was eager to see him because I'd thought he was dead. But you know how hard it is to move in dreams, especially when you're anxious, and by the time I got to the door Lloyd had got tired of waiting and left. In a way, I was glad that Eternity hadn't given him any patience.

Then I dreamed I went to the hospital to look for Lloyd, and there was Homer. He too had developed AIDS, but in the dream I stood by him and cared for him. He was failing, failing, his Fire Island friends weren't there, but at last he knew I loved him truly, and he held me tight and was grateful. Was that a love dream or a hate dream?

IV

TEDDY

18 : THE NEW YEAR'S BABY

The once desert starkness of my burned-out, repainted apartment slowly became overgrown again, with the clutter of new laundry and new old sheet music. It was numbing—every time I turned around, it was Easter, birthday, Christmas. The leaves on Riverside Drive kept turning gold, illuminated at night from within by fluorescent streetlights, like a high-tech stretch of burning bushes. Then they'd disappear, revealing the Hudson and New Jersey briefly, and then incongruously dainty blossoms drew the curtain closed again.

I usually hate New Year's, it's the same old song, but you're supposed to hear new lyrics. Dateless but indifferent—I had money again, and professional confidence—on New Year's Eve I went to a party on the unlucky-but-honest thirteenth floor of an old apartment building, hosted by a perpetual graduate student, a Leeward friend named Nathan Liebmann, who's writing a doctoral dissertation in semiotics that no one, not even he, could describe. Nathan is one of those guys who speaks six languages and insists on doing so. He loves opera, which always eluded me—fake passion passing on a barge—but when he talked about it, it sounded like he was explaining cold fusion.

"Come early, not real late," Nathan had said. "I'm trying to get the decent crowd."

Nathan explained that he had invited a young, curly-haired blond man he had a crush on to the party. "I met Leo at Video Valhalla when I was returning *Death in Venice* and he was returning *Nitty Gritty Gang Bang*." I imagined Nathan writing a paper for his cinema theory seminar: "Art and Porno: Compare and Contrast." "He and his friend are twenty-two, so at least they're legal!"

Anyway, the remake of Tadzio was carrying on at a window, throwing hors d'oeuvres for distance and shouting "Happy fucking New Year" into the night. I didn't like his overbearing manner. It reminded me of the little boy in my namesake's *The Snow Queen,* who's cute but gets a fragment of the devil's mirror in his heart, and it makes him sadistically clever. But I was struck sidelong by the thin blond's quiet, brown-haired buddy. Leo's drunk was animated and wild, whereas his mild companion just grinned tipsily, like the bashful bumpkin mouse in the cartoon who stumbles out of the cider barrel. It was like Beaver and Eddie Haskell. Dondi and Peck's Bad Boy. (See? That's another advantage youngest kids have—we inherit our older siblings' knowledge.) Leo had brought a carton of eggs from the kitchen and started to toss them out the window. He turned fearlessly to me, a stranger to him, and whispered conspiratorially, "*Hen* grenades!"

The brown-haired boy shook his head. "He's embarrassing, isn't he?" He grinned, southern silk in his voice, but he made no move to stop Leo from hurling the eggs.

"Hey, baby! The yolk's on you!" Leo shouted toward the street. He sensed his friend's disapproval and said, "Relax, these aren't actually hitting anybody!"

"What would your mother say?" I joked.

He answered with intelligent but unnerving swiftness. "My mother the lush and her boyfriend the bigger lush—the lusher lush!—were supposed to come visit me over Christmas, but she begged off because of a cold. I don't think she'd care whether I'm throwing eggs, as long as they're not in her martini." His gaze was piercing, like that of a charismatic business lecturer. "What kind of a mother doesn't visit her kid because of a mere fucking cold?"

"Come on, Leo, please don't." Nathan intervened to take the eggs, hesitantly, the way you're reluctant to criticize someone you want to sleep with. "You're an adult now."

"Oooh!" Leo overacted being chastised, took my arm, and whispered into my ear—though we still hadn't been introduced— "You know what Nathan and Nathan's have in common? They're both really old Jewish hot dogs!" He careened off to the kitchen, with his friend giggling behind him, and I remembered the Gilbert and Sullivan lyric about the three little maids from school: *"Everything is a source of fun. Nobody's safe, for we care for none."*

I drank some champagne, girl drink or not. The next time they veered near me, Nathan introduced us. "Leo Trout, Teddy Fife, this is Blue Monahan. He's a pianist."

"I'll bet," Leo leered.

"I said *pianist*," Nathan persisted. "And a songwriter. He wrote that Randy Battles song that was just playing! And the Pow detergent theme! You know, *Pow is the answer.*" Nathan was my best publicist. This last item made Teddy perk up, and I tried to engage him.

"Pow! Wow!"

"Are you a musician, too?" I smiled.

"Well, I started on piano," he answered in a pleasantly straightforward way, "but I didn't have the patience to practice. The key of C was okay, but sharps and flats were too much."

"Well, calling them *accidentals* does make them seem dangerous." I tried not to try too hard. "Is Teddy for Theodore?"

"Uh huh. That means loved by God, or loves God, I forget which. You look like the guy on that TV show." Leo started throwing hors d'oeuvres at people, and Teddy went to defuse him. I asked Nathan about Teddy.

"They're both college dropouts from Kentucky. They wait tables at, what's that tourist trap? Bambino's. Leo's wild, Teddy does damage control. Teddy's a brat, but Leo is fucked up. There's a difference."

"Why do you have a crush on someone who's fucked up?"

He looked at me as if the answer were obvious. "To *save* him."

"No, *you* shut up!" I heard Leo shout at someone. "Just being old enough doesn't automatically make you God!" His belief in pervasive poison reminded me of Lloyd, who hated almost everyone, too, except Lloyd's hatred was moral, spiritual somehow, *arrived at*. Leo didn't object to people, he just didn't care about them.

"Hi! Just me!" Teddy had returned to my side and was grinning shyly. "Leo's got a big mouth! It once got him locked in a car trunk. He announced over a loudspeaker that a guy in our frat was getting married when in fact he'd just been dumped by his girlfriend."

"Yike! He's your best friend?"

"He's my only gay friend. We met the night we were initiated. We barfed on each other."

"Barf brothers, that is a bond."

"After he dropped out, I had no one to hang out with, and he suggested I come here, too. I need suggestions."

"Were you lonely?" I asked him.

Teddy squirmed. Midwesterners think loneliness should be kept to yourself. "I don't know. . . . I just couldn't figure out what to major in. My mom jokes that I should have just dropped out of high school and saved them fifty thousand dollars."

"Well, she jokes. At least, she's being supportive?"

"Oh sure, she worries about New York, though—she and my dad are born again." After saying that, he hastily added, "But don't get the wrong idea. Just because they're religious, they're still really *good* people!" I thought of Jeannie's mom's advice, that if they love their family they can love you.

"And Leo's parents?" He didn't seem to resist my interviewing him.

Teddy shrugged, in Christian nonjudgment. "His poor mom. His dad's a big chain-smoking blowhard, I think. He's trying to get on TV as a family values guy, even though he's divorced? I guess that doesn't count against you now. He actually *forbade* Leo to move here, he said a son in New York would be a liability! So if they ever find out he's gay, he would be really fucked! In the bad sense!"

"Couldn't they accept him?"

"Well, his dad yells about love, but I think he just likes yelling. He's like a Vegas act. Leo would kill me for talking about him."

"Shall we have some more bubbly, then?"

"Sure, I'll go with the flow." He seemed to imprint on me, relieved if someone else made the decisions.

After that things got fuzzy, though I remember hearing Leo shout, "Stop liking my friend!"

To my happy surprise, Teddy magically appeared, like the New Year's baby dropped by the stork, in my bed the next morning. He was still asleep when I awoke and saw him, his cheeks and lips puffed like those of a doll awaiting a bottle. For a moment I was frightened, remembering an experience from my Wild Rover days—not the much-joked-about fright of waking up with a monster but the more depressing fright of waking up with a young beauty, who woke up and was terrified to find himself with monster me. It was like those trick-ending horror stories, where the narrator who's afraid of ghosts realizes *he's* the ghost. However, when Teddy awoke, his eyes brightened and he slowly grinned.

"Hi!" he managed to whisper. "I can't believe I let myself go!"

"Nice to have you. Happy new year."

He leaned over and kissed me, then closed his eyes again. After a minute he said, "I'm not a tramp or anything. This has never happened to me before."

I rubbed my temples. "And what, uh, happened?"

"Well, at midnight you said I was the most beautiful thing you'd ever seen, and you asked if you could kiss me, and then you actually picked me up and gave me the kiss of all time!"

"Yikes! I apologize!"

"Are you kidding? It was wonderful. Nobody's ever kissed me like that before. And then you asked to do the same thing at one a.m. and at two a.m.—and then we came here."

I brought him some juice, and we met each other again. He had been in New York barely a month. I was intrigued by the fact that he was born the year "Love Is the Answer" was a hit. "Maybe it was playing on the radio when your folks conceived you!" I joked.

"Don't make me picture that!" he shuddered.

I saw my own idealized midwestern decency in Teddy. As a child he'd gone to Central America with his parents to help re-build churches there after an earthquake, and as a teen in his hometown of Luxor, he'd joined a church youth group called True Love Waits, all intentional virgins. "We promised to save ourselves for marriage!" He grinned. "It was a whole lot easier for me than for the other guys!" He'd dropped out of Buckeye State, and although it is way at the bottom of Ohio, on the Kentucky border, that still made him partly from my home state, and, any-way, Kentucky is even more sentimental a concept than Ohio. With that added southern liqueur, it must be more wholesome than gray, metallic Cleveland! Stephen Foster suffered there. And, of course, Buckeye is where Red went.

19 : MY LOVER, THE VIRGIN

Teddy and Leo shared a tiny, dark studio apartment that faced a brick wall. Teddy complained about Leo's slovenly habits constantly, but when I suggested he talk about it with Leo, Teddy demurred. "I just can't. It's not my way to complain." No wonder Teddy instantly turned to spending every night with me.

New Year's night, we had a dreamlike first-and-a-half date. Teddy brought a sack of leftover cookies from Bambino's, and we went down to the Battery, where they'd pitched a circus tent with the Statue of Liberty visible in its background. Le Cirque du Nouveau Monde is one of those *nouvell vaudevilles* that don't use animals, but they do feel free to exploit the audience. A clown who didn't use makeup picked Teddy from the audience—probably because he was so adorable the rest of the crowd had to root for him—and tried to coax him to undress. I think it had to do with auditioning a new circus strongman. Teddy was a mortified good sport about it, but I felt eerie watching him take his shirt and, after the clown insisted, his pants off in front of a thousand people. He was wearing boxers, so it wasn't as shocking as briefs would have been, but you had to salute his pliability. When he returned to his seat, to thunderous applause from people who'd escaped his fate, he buried his face on my chest.

We spent that night with my arms around him, my chest to his back, my lips to his nape, two stacked spoons, a completed set, a play fortress of flesh, and I revisited the work-study heaven of being needed. Naughton LeBlanc, the mad virtual therapist I'd visited after Homer exploded on me, was convinced my loneliness came from a desire to re-merge with my twin back to a single cell, but when I pointed out that non-twins, in fact, everybody, wanted sexual merging, he just sort of stared at me and said, "Why are you *resisting* my suggestion?"

Teddy and I seemed naturally at ease with each other. He was ingenuous and I was just no-frills. After all the ambition and covert agendas of Homer's world, Teddy seemed the opposite— gentle and accessible, if inclined to nap. In fact, I mentally listed the lucky differences between them. Teddy, unlike Homer, was satisfied to shop at the Gap and ate diner food without thinking it was funny. In fact, he was afraid of sushi. He had no particular ambitions, which was relaxing for me. Instead of a sleazy bar, we met through friends at an Ivy League party. Instead of obfuscatory brown, his eyes were a transparent blue. Homer sent his shirts out; Teddy washed and ironed his own. Again, I'm assuming God does symbolism. Homer was exotic heights, Teddy was homespun. The vamp and the farm girl. Circe and Penelope.

Teddy didn't care about bodybuilding. He had skinny arms and a soft belly, and barely needed to shave. Instead of a hundred-dollar haircut, he wore the hemispherical bangs pioneer boys used to get from bowls on their heads. Lucky for him, the Shemp look was big that year. True, he had no hobbies, no direction, and he gave the impression of simplemindedness with my friends because he'd be silent around them, like the magic frog in the cartoon who only sings when it's alone with its owner. But he had a still center which I thought was wisdom. The kind New York doesn't know to value.

And, unlike Homer, who was constantly eager to be "arrested," Teddy was sexually inexperienced, fond of kissing but otherwise silent and limp, like an opossum being examined by a bear. After a few nights together, I asked him if he wanted to progress.

"Have you ever had a serious relationship before?"

"Sure, for almost a week."

"Well, I mean, do you want to progress to a more physical level?"

"Please, Blue, I am terrified of AIDS. I've been hearing about it all my life. I could never relax and have sex, not even safe sex, something might go wrong."

"I thought you said you'd had a relationship."

"Just flirting. I had roommates."

"Well, I love being with you. We don't have to have literal sex."

"Oh thank you!" He beamed, and kissed me passionately.

So, we limited our lovemaking to cuddling. I suggested fantasy wordplay, but it embarrassed him, and it's true that if you consider pornography for more than a second, it turns truly silly. So, we were *sweethearts*, not lovers—but I was proud of that. It proved my honor, my strength, my *classiness*, that I could love sincerely enough to share a bed happily with someone who preferred chastity. I wasn't the cruel owner here, and the hovering awareness of fatal illness everywhere made it seem like a true lover's bid to honor and protect his love. Besides, okay, whenever I did try anything, he'd say, "You're relentless," as a tribute and put-down, and briefly turn over.

Holding Teddy as he slept, a doting, downy duckling, I thought of the first man I'd gone home with—I couldn't yet say no, I'd been raised to be obliging, and a mayoral assistant who was running for Caesar basically demanded I join him. At his place he started calling me a bitch and clearly forgot he was with another human once he started groaning, like mining equipment working against a deadline. Now I had become that man, and this was my chance to prove myself better.

Despite that curb, we walked without umbrellas in the rain across the park, to find the Frick museum closed, and we didn't even mind. We walked all over the city's neighborhoods, each delightful to fresh eyes, like kingdoms in Disneyland. The dazzling, hopeful upsurgence of the Wall Street skyline, at least as seen from the Brooklyn Bridge, the ornate, filthy alleyways of Chinatown, the lavishly empty showrooms of SoHo, Riverside Park at sunset with the George Washington Bridge glittering in the distance, all were new to Teddy, and so, newly thrilling to me, to be his decent docent. *Welcome to Baghdad, kid!* That's right, roll the Happiness Montage again. Basically, just screen the first one again, and loosen the focus.

Besweatered Teddy laughed commonsensically at the black-clothed, tattooed East Villagers: "That girl with the ring in her nose! Wait till she has to blow it! They're like kids playing pirates! As if life didn't serve enough trouble—they have to draw demons and skeletons on the walls!" As our relationship firmed, we spoke of going to clean places, the Grand Canyon and Hawaii, too. He said what I longed for him to say—"Blue, I want to see everything beautiful with you as my guide!"

I was careful to take it easy this time, and to take sincerity checks as we waded deeper. I tried pacing things with nights off, but he always called me late, asking to come stay with me, and I liked it. One sundae of a Sunday, we were watching the Lincoln Center fountain unaccountably flourish and ebb, and I mentioned, "I could get serious here, Teddy. What do you think?"

"I'm willing if you are. I don't feel any gulf between us at all. It's as if you're my own age!" he said excitedly. "I'm happy when I'm with you. Every day is Valentine's Day!" Teddy developed a newcomer's enthusiasm for lobbing loaded sweetmeats like I Love You and I Miss You over the phone, too. He even reassured me that he liked my thinning hair.

"I wish mine were thinning! It's so hard to brush!"

"Well, I'll try to think of it this way—I'm just getting taller than my hair."

Lurking in this enchanted wood, of course, was Leo, who got distraught if Teddy and I walked hand in hand, and shouted, "Stop loving my friend in public!" I tried to win his approval, but he felt he had dibs on Teddy, whom he'd summoned to New York to keep him company. He chilled me with his comments about having to wait on old people, blacks, and Jews at Bambino's, though he admired well-dressed customers, and I wondered if his hometown was like Petty. I'm perplexed by homosexuals who are bigots themselves, so frightened they have to shore up status to buffer themselves from self-hatred. Actually, it's a heterosexual epidemic, too. It occurred to me that Leo's values, Hollywood's, and the Fire Island Pines' were all the same—those of high school.

When Lent began, Teddy found out his parents were coming to visit from Luxor. There was a burned-out church in Harlem they were going to help rebuild. Teddy hadn't told them he was gay, despite his mother's repeated leading end-of-phone-call question, "Is there anything you'd like to tell me?" This haunted me when Teddy told me, "I hate gay men. But I don't think of you as a gay man," or when he heard his voice on my phone machine tape and gasped, "Oh, God, I sound like a . . . southern . . . *fag!*" I can see why gay partnerships are so unstable—with no children or family support to bind them in others' eyes, they're like trying to produce a long-running TV series without sponsors or an audience.

Teddy made a tagboard sign to greet his parents at the airport: WELCOME MOM & DAD. In case they didn't recognize him, I guess. It was an unembarrassed gesture of flat-out family love that sophisticates cringe at, but I took the sign as a good sign. When they arrived, they were the ruddy, round, exuberant county fairgoers Crawford had sneered about on Fire Island. They were remarkably young, too—just over forty, I figured, married right out of high school, maybe because of an imminent Teddy. I was also impressed that this long-wed couple walked hand in hand, and teased each other physically. She tousled his hair, he patted her fanny. "Loving background," I noted mentally. "Jackpot!"

I played tour guide, which was fine until I nervously got lost with them in the Central Park Ramble. There's a Bad Dream Walking for you—lost in the woods in the middle of Manhattan with your lover's parents. It panicked me that they wouldn't think much of me as a protector of their son, or whoever they thought I was. His dad joked about sending up flares, but the orienting towers of the Beresford, like a landmark mesa, finally rescued us.

On Columbus Avenue, while Teddy and his mom browsed imitation funny T-shirts for gifts for congregation members back home, his dad innocently asked me, "Are you married, yourself?"

I tried to guess at an honest, harmless answer. "No, but two of my brothers are," I said compulsively, as if I might get partial credit for that.

"Did they like me?" I asked Teddy after they'd returned to Harlem.

"Yes," he answered mildly. "Mom asked me if you were my best friend."

"Well, that sounds like a sign she gets the picture."

"I told her you were. You and Leo."

20 : POLICEMAN, SAVE MY CHILD

I got what hipper people could call a gig without giggling, performing my songs at the Keyboard Room, and Teddy attended every night. In fact, the manager there mistook him for a new employee, and Teddy had obligingly brought ice water to some customers before they realized the confusion. He went with the flow, even if it wasn't good for him. I'd offered Leo free seats, but he never responded. Teddy always sat alone and hid his face whenever I dedicated a song to him, even though I wasn't so trophy mad as to point him out.

Reed Vogel, whom I'd let drift out of the picture after I met Teddy, hobbled up to congratulate me after one show. He was very thin, but he smiled broadly.

"Reed! What are you doing here?" He'd startled me. "I mean, how did you even know this was going on?"

"It was in the papers, Blooey!" I forgot I had been listed. "Is that boy at the bar who you dedicated the love song to?"

"Reed, I can't deny it." I felt hotly embarrassed, a heel with enough morals to feel guilty. "I mean, I did say that I wouldn't, I mean, you knew I didn't dare . . . to get serious with you."

"Yes, you tortured man!" he teased. "I understand. You found someone to actually sleep with."

"Well, actually, it's someone else not to."

He crossed his eyes to indicate life was cuckoo. "He's certainly cute. You deserve it, Blooey! Anyway, I should go, you have other people who want to greet you." He graciously withdrew to rejoin what looked like two stewardesses in street clothes, and Kip Lastly, my former Telemachus, stepped in to pump my hand.

He was with the tiniest woman you ever barely saw. "My fiancée, Tina!" he announced happily. "We met doing Dopey and Sleepy!"

She picked up the rest of his speech like they were already long married. "In Disney on Parade!" she added helpfully. I wondered who had played which.

"Congratulations!" I was moved by Kip's relieved expression, no more wandering unproven, mistaken for a schoolboy. "What next?"

"Back on tour! As Tweedledum and Tweedledee!" He'd found his twin, she was even smaller than he, and they had their work to share.

That night, as Teddy and I headed home, we heard gunshots, and when we reached my corner, police and spectators swarmed around its deli. One of the clerks, whom I knew by face, had been shot in a botched robbery, and we unexpectedly saw the body emerge on a gurney between the avenues of brightly bundled fresh flowers. It was momentary, a sheet quickly covered it. Teddy had never seen death before, and he clung to me more tightly that night.

It occurred to me that Teddy looked like the boy in a picture that had hung in our house, a barefoot boy carrying his fishing pole over a fragile little bridge, and a barely smiling guardian angel, great and able, following invisibly to protect him. It's a dangerous world, people get shot and, just as awfully, worn away. I wanted to make sure this sweet guy had a wonderful life. It would give my life meaning, and his support. Was that imperialism? Was my brain doing a public relations job for my penis? Lloyd's old criticism haunted me—"Boo Hoo, you just want to romp in the meadows of fresh, smooth, childish flesh, as if kissing it could save you from complication and death!"

Still, I had been a troubled kid. Now I wanted to do my best to save Teddy from that trouble. I wanted to rescue someone like Dad had rescued that woman in the candy store.

I felt almost fictional in my newfound security. Then the law of averages summoned me for discomfort duty. I was shopping for a wedding gift for newly engaged Lulu at the sleepy boutiques in the West Village, and I had just bought her a blender—she'd always said daiquiris symbolized elegant happiness. Sunset highlighted the ivy-grizzled brick side street, a golden gravy on the visual feast, and suddenly I ran into Homer. It was as if he were only physically manifested in seductive settings—like, you'd never see him at the Department of Motor Vehicles—and I was surprised at my own apprehensiveness, like getting a marine physical sprung on you at age forty, but I reminded myself that I had a devoted and comprehensible beau napping at my apartment.

Why couldn't he have grown a beard, I wished, and dismantled my desire for him? But no, there were those cheeks, those lost fields of home. And instead of being icy, Homer had progressed to being casually warm.

"You great big hunk of He-hood!" he exclaimed—lovers' talk so inflated it's devalued, the kind salesmen lavish on clients. "I thought of you—I walked past your building a few weeks ago with a good friend of mine."

That's right, keep it mysterious. "And did you point it out with great sentimental reverence?" I asked, humorously, I hoped.

Homer hesitated at my half joke. "Well . . . I pointed it out," he said with teasing flatness. Then he added, "Naaw. . . . Actually, I didn't even point it out!"

He grinned but saw my face fall. "Aww, Blue, I love teasing you, you are so hilariously sensitive!" He touched my arm, a jolt whose voltage he may not have realized.

"You look good—like the movie version of yourself!" I smiled. *Demonstrate your sanity.* "You're prospering?"

"Yep, while I can. Got to while you can."

Vagueness usually signals a will to end a conversation. I grasped for safe subjects. "How's your dad?"

"Fine. The folks are fine."

"Folks? Didn't you say your mom was, uh, dead?"

"Oh right." He paused. "My dad and stepmother, I mean. He remarried. Nice woman."

My game piece kept sliding back to square one. This was my last chance before the crystal again grew clouded. "So . . . any time-ripened insights into what happened between us?"

"Aww, no, Blue. You're the insightful one. I just . . . don't ever think about it."

I never could help trying to file my feelings at the Love Library. "I did think it would be my happiness to make you happy."

He smiled again, his crooked smile, like he was either pained or bitterly amused, receiving an unsought award with postage due, and he glanced to his side, as if he were about to cheat at cards. "It's all timing." He sighed and surveyed the shifting light on a flock of pigeons circling in the sky to the west, their wings like one great, rippling banner, now gold, now silver as the sunset beneath struck them in their indecisive-looking rotation. "It's not enough to meet Mr. Right. It's got to be at the Right Time. I wasn't ready for you then."

I shivered, as the past's crowded subway went rattling through me.

"You should get a dog," Homer continued. "I think of you as a Dog Person."

I know he meant well, but I imagined myself as a sodden, unkempt half human from the Island of Lost Souls.

"You're seeing someone now?" I asked instinctively.

"Well, at this very moment, you're who I'm seeing."

"You know what I mean."

"Yup. And the answer is, yup," he spoke softly, volunteering no details. He didn't return the question, either. Good taste or indifference?

"Well, he better be good to you," I said.

"Blue, you are the last of your species! You always make me feel good." He smiled. "Well, he's German, not as tender as you, but you know me, you know my excess baggage better than anyone." I didn't think I knew it at all. "I don't always want what's good for me. I'm a complex person."

I wondered why he complimented me so, as if only some external force kept him from loving me. He had always cited his complexity as if it closed all debate, like James Bond's license to kill.

"You deserve someone who cares about your happiness." I pitched myself ritually, knowing there was no negotiation to follow, helplessly steering into the skid of my aching sweet tooth for him. Beauty Fool. Besides, I had someone, didn't I? Our encounter felt illusory in this floorless moment, more rerun than live.

"You can't go back," Homer recited sagely. "You always have to go on . . . to someone new." His wisdom took on a tinge of the promiscuous there, of one most used to being the thrilling stranger. The setting sun lit his face now, gloriously as a cherub, though with a touch of worldly pain that excused all, and we contemplated each other, fearfully or fondly, who knows? Besides the momentary gold in his brown hair, I saw tiny streaks of veteran's gray at his temples, and incongruously, in his delinquent's sideburns—rain clouds in heaven.

"I'm overdue at a We Love Us gala," he said smoothly. "Though I'll just be an extra at this one." Even on the street, he was the host and I the guest. He held my hand and volunteered a long, tender parting kiss, the familiar milk and pepper taste. When I felt it expanding into tongue territory, or, all right, when I expanded it, he followed along, either from dormant passion sneaking an uncomplicated free sample or from his passive will to let the situation float past without a scene. Salesmen are compelled to please, and maybe a French kiss seemed a small community service for old crimes. Was I being merely randy, or punitive, or desperate, or is it possible a capsule replay of our relationship was appropriate? It was delicious while it lasted, as any last meal should be.

He smiled but enacted stern eyebrows. "Your mama didn't feed you enough!"

"No." I tried to grin. "She let me get too used to All I Could Eat."

"I'll remember this," Homer said, touched my lips, and tapped his head. "I am a camera!" He turned and headed toward the real sunset as his unreal cowboy legend would have it.

I didn't know what to say, but brandished Lulu's gift. "I . . . am a blender!"

Bittersweet after this encounter, I impulsively went and bought Teddy a needlessly expensive set of gold designer silverware, even though I'd mocked it when he admired it in a shop the previous week. The pieces had twig-shaped handles. I had said they looked hard to hold. Teddy seemed to love them, though, and was surprised to the point of hiccups. He promised to make me a fancy dinner.

21 : A TRIUMPH IN A TEAPOT

Mom was set upon by a pack of illnesses—heart, lung, and stomach problems that waged three-ring mayhem inside her. Megan took a leave of absence from her school to go to Cleveland, and, since I had no job to leave, I went to Cleveland to bear crucial, useless witness at the hospital. The doctors were steady as newscasters as they theorized what would kill her first, while on the walls around us hung cut-out Easter decorations of newborn bunnies and chicks leaping from their shells with clearly no idea of what life held in store.

The intensity of the intensive-care unit saturated everything with a surreal stress, having to brace yourself every day for the helpless spectacle, the automated mock-pinewood doors swinging open on your arrival like the gates of hell's rec room, where the devil dandled Mom in a cat's cradle net of tubing. She couldn't speak, and her eyes glittered like an animal's in a trap. Megan brought her paper and pen as we made upbeat small talk about the spaghetti dinner Lulu had cooked for everyone the night before. "Imagine, Mom, loony Lulu cooking dinner for twenty!"

Slowly, laboriously, and almost illegibly, Mom wrote in a slant that wound precipitously down the page, You . . . kids . . . always . . . liked . . . spaghetti.

We all laughed like it was an inspired Oscar acceptance speech, and then Mom slowly scribbled further questions. *What time is it? . . . Where are the grandkids? . . . Who's cooking for Dad?* I guess he was alive again in her mind. *Where is my wedding ring?* She'd been afraid it would be stolen while she was unconscious, and she'd asked George to put it in the family safe deposit box. *What is my room number? . . . How many rooms in this hospital?* We didn't know. *That nurse looks familiar. Did her family go to St. Vitus's?* Yes, she was right.

The younger old woman in the next bed could talk, and she kept repeating over and over, like a parrot, "Who are you? Is she your mother? How old are you? How old is she? Are you my children? Are you my father?"

Mom began to recover, but excruciatingly, and she became more confused. She kept pulling out her IV the way Lloyd had at the end, and trying to stand and walk around. She kept muttering that the library would be robbed or she needed to make dinner. They finally had to strap her down and put mittens on her hands, which frustrated her, the Born Leader. She did not want to resign her office, she was determined to live to see every one of us married. She was determined to live to see every grandchild marry. She was determined to live to see every great-grandchild marry. She wanted to live to see the whole story to its ever-expanding conclusion, which isn't even possible in fiction.

She did pull through, with the emphasis on *pull,* or, anyway, she was discharged. She could barely walk, but it was her triumph in a teapot to be back at home, her one reality, the ancestral center of her empire. I stayed with her and Lulu for a few days. For the first time in that house, I had a room to myself. Lulu giggled with guilt when she discovered Mom had managed to bring home a sackful of hospital silverware and drinking glasses as well. Shoring up supplies for the tomb, sandbagging against night, restitution for life itself.

Mom started making long lists, categorizing all the objects in the house and constantly writing down the time of day. She saved eggshells and used tissue as if for reference purposes. It was the sort of librarian-gone-haywire behavior that had driven Lulu to a fury when she was the last child living at home, but now she tolerated it impassively. Mom would pause in her list making and stare as if at a distant vista, distracted, like she had to finish a task in order to break the spell. There was a byzantine Last Days in the Bunker feel among the piles of old newspaper and expired coupons, relieved only by nightly I Miss You calls from Teddy, devotedly polishing love's already sparkling chalice. Lulu raised her eyebrows after the third call and said, "You've met someone, too? And here I thought you and I were doomed." It was a disturbing way to express hope.

I was packing my suitcase to go back to New York when I noticed with a start that the magazines I'd brought with me were missing. I didn't care about the copies of *Songwriter* or *Showbiz Now*, but I had brought along what is tactfully called a male pictorial, *Hollywood Bottom Boys*. I felt that jolt I had when Mom had caught me masturbating, because I'd never come out to her in so many words.

"Lulu, did you borrow some magazines from my suitcase?" I took her aside to ask.

"No, I haven't been anywhere near your dumb suitcase," she said defensively, a touch of her old, lonely contention resurfacing. "Talk to Light-fingered Lil."

Mom was sitting innocently in the kitchen, carefully and repeatedly jotting down her name. The electric clock over her head buzzed gratingly. It used to be soundless, but I guess the warranty had expired.

"Um, Mom, I was wondering if you'd borrowed some magazines from my room?"

"Let me think. No. . . . Oh! Yes. I borrowed your show-business magazines. Very interesting." She seemed bland about it, limper than in her grand marshal days.

"Well, they didn't surprise you or anything?"

"No. I'm a grown-up." It was weird, a veiled discussion of pornography with my mother.

"Then, you understand about me."

"God made a lot of different people." She sighed. "You're not hurting anyone." She looked out the window, where next door one of the middle-aged Lannigan sons was unloading a case of Pepsis. "It was Pepsi for breakfast that put that bunch on the wrong track," she reflected. One of them had been killed in a barroom fight, and, worse in Mom's eyes, another had been born again.

"I do want you to know, I'm HIV negative. I'm in good health."

"I did worry about that," she said slowly, and grew general again. "I just wanted happiness for all of you." She was using the past tense. "Twelve Christmas stockings, twelve Easter baskets." She forgot my favorite, twelve jack-o'-lanterns lined up on the porch. Even after Jock died. A Halloween memorial.

"Anyway . . . I'm the same person I always was. I am trying to lead a decent life."

"Like I told you as kids. There are good and bad white people, there are good and bad black people. The same . . . is true . . . here."

She held my hand, with surprising firmness for someone so frail, or perhaps I was surprised at the dramatic gesture.

"When God sent me twins," she said yearningly, "I wondered if he was sending me you to make up for the loss of John."

I was moved, involuntarily, like a ghostly occupied elevator had passed through me, and then I thought, John *who*?

Then I remembered John was Jock's real name—for St. John of the Cross, or John the Evangelist, or else for one of the actors who played Tarzan, the record is hazy. And then I remembered that Jock was still alive when we were born, so I guess Mom thought God was making up for the tragic thing He intended to do later. I guess she didn't statistically hold any of her miscarriages against God. In her illness the past was becoming dreamlike, without strict chronology, and, from a woman who had always calculated grandchildren's relative birth dates like a fan might baseball data, it seemed an eerie sign of surrender. She was slowly becoming transparent, gradually joining the caravan of ghosts, her dead mother and father, her sister who found it all too much to bear, Dad, Jock, all of life's miscarriages, sailing away before my eyes.

I got back to New York for my next Keyboard Room gig, and a few nights later my phone was ringing when I came in late. The message machine flashed. Teddy, who didn't like to answer my phone, was sitting in the living room looking pale. "It's been ringing all night," he said nervously. I answered the phone.

"Blue?" Red's voice was dry as parchment. If there was ever any telepathy between us, it was at that moment. He had just told me that Mom had died. Teddy knew instantly and clutched me. That Adults Only thrill ride—did I still want it?

All her graying children gathered in Cleveland for the unmooring, for our somber shift into orphanhood. Mom had always been the plump, unvarnished granny, but after her final weight loss and the makeup they put on her, I was astonished at how beautiful she looked in her coffin, candlelit like a sleeping princess, weirdly like Judy, like the striking, hopeful girl in the honeymoon photos I'd seen. Kitty, Megan, and Judy sang "Wayfaring Stranger" at the service. It's more gospel than Catholic, but its sad happiness gripped me.

> *I'm just a goin' over Jordan,*
> *I'm just a goin' over home.*

Jeannie came with Red from California, and, to my surprise, normally squeamish Teddy asked to come with me. "It isn't like a hospital," he reasoned. "It's just a funeral." Despite the grief and the harsh sense of time's nonsensical rush, having all the siblings in one place felt like a defiant union against all that. And in bringing Teddy with me, I found a new sense of belonging, and no one, not even George, seemed to blink at my unconventional partner. If success can change your race, or the way people see you, maybe my recent sane success made my unorthodoxies beside the point.

Conal couldn't help laughing involuntarily when it dawned on him what was going on, but when I must have looked hurt, he hastily touched the tip of his nose to indicate he wanted to talk to me. While Teddy modestly chatted with Red, Conal shrugged. "Hey, whatever turns your turbines! Your, uh, friend reminds me of that yawning kid in pajamas, with the auto tire! In the old ad? Remember, 'Time to Re-tire'? Or else the Big Boy statue, the striped kid bringing the tray of burgers!"

"That's him, in fact, Conal."

We laughed and then shared a silence. Usually insincere for fun's sake, Conal's merely friendly voice then chilled me. "But . . . he is awful young!"

Red restored my confidence when he said, "Well, Co-zygote, I get a really good feeling about that Teddy guy. Son of church builders. Puts himself down, I like that in a man. No practical skills. You seem well-matched." In the midst of our dark clothes and our shaken sense of mortality, I felt that equally serious gravity that attends a happy ending.

22 : AWFUL YOUNG

Teddy seemed depressed after the burial, though. When we returned to New York, I suggested he move in with me, since his clothes and belongings were strewn all over my apartment anyway. For the first time, there was a disquieting quiet between us. Teddy didn't answer, the pause was a lonesome highway, and he half-closed his eyes like he did when counting his spare change. Finally, laconically, he changed the subject. "I have to get a real job first." He sighed. Infatuation's hectic song had taken its first pause for breath. The perpetual motion machine had had its first brownout.

A few days later, to cheer him up and boost my image in his eyes, I took him to a party VH1 threw for Randy Battles in somebody's penthouse. TV cameras crowded the entrance as we squeezed past the infotainers trying to interview the sequin-sheathed starlets, and Teddy was clearly self-conscious about his polo shirt and jeans.

"I'm going to go get a free drink," he whispered and slipped into the recesses of the reception.

Jostled by other arriving guests, I slipped to the side and overheard one record exec faking having fun with another. "I hope you haven't heard this one: Do women really have orgasms?"

"I give up," his male colleague answered. "Do they?"

The joke teller grinned. "*Who cares?*"

Both men laughed, and when Teddy wandered back with his bourbon and Coke, I felt deeply proud of my self-restraint, and of him, knowing he was the purest creature in this den of weasels. Randy came over to meet us and asked Teddy what he did.

"I'm a . . . waiter?" Teddy answered, as if it were a question, or a tentative answer pending Randy forgiving its humbleness.

"Well, tonight you're gonna get waited *on!*" Randy grinned, gesturing to the circulating caterers, and pumped Teddy's hand, even though his gaze was already distracted by a potentate over my shoulder. "And what else do you do, or want to do?"

Teddy grinned at the floor. "I'm devoting myself to Blue."

I was thrilled at Teddy's forthrightness, but it was lost in the mundane buzz around us, and Randy's concentration had already moved on. "Great!" he bayed.

"Randy, what are the odds on another Grammy?" whoever it was called.

"Jay, I won last year! Now they have to punish me for my big head! Hey, Manfred, my man!" Randy proceeded down the non-linear receiving line to greet another executive I didn't recognize, doing what Sonny LaMatina used to call "bowing to Decca." I reflected that successes—country-western stars, athletes, politicians, whoever—share the necessary skill of a tireless, convincing interest in strangers.

Teddy seemed self-conscious and drank more bourbon and Cokes. While waiting for him to return from a bathroom visit, I saw Milla Korones across the room, grinning and ablaze in blue sequins like the Mediterranean in midafternoon.

"Blue, how wonderful to see you!" She beamed, which I took to mean I was seeing her at a wonderful time. "I'm getting married!"

I was happy for her, she'd been a buffeted vessel. "Ithaca at last!" I laughed. "Is he in showbiz?"

"No, thank God!" she blurted, like it was a prize-winning answer. "I mean, not really. Russell's a sound man."

"Well, I should hope so."

"I mean, he's a sound engineer. He worked on Randy's album! On your song!"

"And that's my sweetheart, over there getting the drink!"

"Blue, he's adorable!"

We embraced and yelled like we'd just won the game show. My favorite: Communion. The party had gotten loud, and our overacting went unnoticed. Her Russell called for her, and Teddy came unsteadily back, his tipsiness a gesture of surrender and defiance at once.

"The bartender told me I looked Oriental!" he slurred grumpily as he leaned into my side. I could see that, what with his dark brown bangs, smooth skin, and habitually downcast eyes, but I knew this wasn't the moment to explain it—and Teddy always complained when I explained others' behavior instead of just getting mad at them for his sake.

"Maybe he meant to say you looked *ornamental!*" I improvised, but it was an accidentally inflammatory whimsy. Teddy bristled and turned away from me, knowing the power of withholding his gaze.

"That's all I am, isn't it? Decoration. No special talent. I'm the only person here I've never heard of!" He sulked and walked away, out onto the terrace. Homer was put off by my failure, and here Teddy was put off by my success.

I followed him out there, where a breeze tousled his hair as if to calm him, and beneath us a thousand lights twinkled, troubled lives seen from an enchanting distance.

"You're my superstar," I told him. "You're better than all these ruined people! Haven't I tried to be good to you? Don't I always ask you if you're getting what you want?"

"Well . . . yes."

"But you have to tell me what you want. I can't always read your mind."

The wind petted him more effectively than I could, and he sighed at the luscious night. "Okay. I'll try. No one ever asked me to communicate before." He paused. "There is something I want to tell you, Blue," he said gravely.

"What?" I asked, sensing his uneasiness.

"Last night . . . you snored."

Silence hung in the air like an inside-out laugh track.

"Is that it?" I exhaled finally. No one else had ever said I snored. Was I aging? Still, what a relief, if this was my worst marital sin. "Well, I have a cold, my nose was stuffed up. You snore, too, when you've drunk too much. It's sweet."

"I don't snore, Blue."

"Anyway, my mom used to say she missed my dad's snoring. She said it proved he was there."

"I'm not your wife."

Another ill-advised improv. "I'm not saying that. I'm just trying to be friendly and anecdotal."

"Well, don't try so hard."

Teddy had another bourbon and Coke, and although he danced with me when the party got wilder, he seemed drowsy, shaking his head absentmindedly, a toddler in a funny home video who's prematurely high on disco, a sleeper turning in his bed, a dreamer flinching. It didn't seem fair to dance with him if he wasn't actually there, so I took him back home. It was only a few blocks from the penthouse to my walk-up, but it reminded me that distance in Manhattan is as much vertical as horizontal.

"There's something else," he muttered, as I walked him up the stairs. "Not just snoring. . . . Last night, when you asked to beat off while we were kissing?"

"Yeah?" I sometimes did this—it was our approximation of sex—but I always asked him first.

"When you came, you got come on me." He never spoke this frankly when he was sober.

"But it was just on your stomach, we cleaned it up."

"I don't care, it's gross, not to mention scary. Don't come anymore."

The second we got inside the door, Teddy stumbled to the toilet and started to vomit—he had still had that much self-control on our walk home—but I held him, and undressed him, and stood in the shower with him, and put him to bed, and then cleaned up the bathroom. The next morning, he was contrite and thanked me for being so good to him, and we both brushed our teeth and kissed, in our hastily sweetened way, heady and desperate, jungle adventurers who'd just survived a dangerous pass.

"I love you." I touched his nose playfully. He rubbed it reflexively.

"I know," he answered, and then, faintly, added, "I love you too."

23 : CRY, CRY AGAIN

August arrived again, and I went to another family wedding, Lulu's, which seems in retrospect like defying the Homer curse, only this time in West Virginia. The country roads were timeless, trees and hills piled like frayed pillows against the horizon, with here and there a cable TV radar dish the size of a Ferris wheel. It must have been economically depressed, though, because I passed a lot of roadside yard sales, toys and dishes, family belongings displayed as if a twister had carried off the house but left the contents behind.

The church basement reception featured a homemade wedding cake that jokingly sported a bride and groom in a model race car, and waggish Conal joked about the joke by removing the groom from the driver's seat and putting him under the car's wheels, with some ketchup for gore. Conal's freckled face and jokes were fun when he was a teenager, but now, with him nearing fifty, they resemble an overripe banana. And of course Lulu was upset about ketchup on the cake, never mind the added sour emotional condiments.

. . .

It had been a record heat wave in New York, and, when I got back to my apartment, Teddy was lounging in his boxers with Leo Trout. It was very hot and humid, despite the electric fan—I'd never gotten around to air conditioning, Mom thought it was *spoiled,* like color television. Both of them were drenched and drunk, and Leo had his shirt off, too, and I noticed with suppressed fright that his skinny torso was covered with scars. Several were operation scars, but others were inexplicable, though they looked like cigarette burns.

"How was your brunch shift?"

Teddy was irritable. "Ugh! Hell plus! The fizz went out of the Coke machine! The air conditioning broke! Half the staff got food poisoning at the same party last night and couldn't work! It was insane!"

"We had a busload of old people who were headed to see some goddam musical you probably wrote!" slurred Leo. "Old people are the worst! *The* worst customers."

Teddy seemed sickened by the heat and announced curtly, "Don't worry, it's our own beer! We bought it!" Leo whispered something in his ear, and then he giggled and whispered something back. I was being pointedly ignored in my own home.

"You want to share with the rest of the class?" I tried.

Teddy shook his head vigorously, as if to change stations. "Blue, we have to talk," he said. "You are the nicest guy I ever met, and I don't want to hurt you . . . but I have to tell you, it's too much for me, I've been feeling overwhelmed. I don't feel comfortable in this relationship anymore." He actually announced this with Leo sitting at his side, and from his innocent mouth his words eerily echoed Homer's. Here it came again. The old male story—antsy in the pants. The Seven-Month Itch—that's the Seven-Year Itch calculated in New York minutes. Leo stared at the ceiling to simulate absence. I actually had to ask him to leave so Teddy and I could talk.

"You didn't do anything wrong, Blue," he began, after Leo left smirking with discomfort. "If anything, you were too good.

You were so encouraging, so supportive—it made me think, do you know who I am? I don't know why you treat me as if I were special. I'm not, I flunked out of school, you act like I'm wonderful, and I don't see how I can be—it makes me think you're crazy or something."

"But you're a good person, you're still finding yourself. I'll see you through!"

"I'm not your petting zoo, I'm not your pet project, I'm not a child. Ow!" He paused to scratch several mosquito bites on his bare legs. "I'm not good like you say, or, anyway, I don't want to be good all the time. When I'm mad at someone, I don't want you to try to talk me out of it. I want you to be mad, too. I just need to relax, to be with people my own age. People who aren't dying!"

This did not feel good, being punished for suffering. "But you never complained, and I'd do anything to make you happy."

"I know that, Blue, I feel that coming at me. I just . . . don't . . . desire you anymore. Six months with just one person is an awfully long time."

Desire—the non-negotiable clause. The fizz had gone out of our Coke machine. "But . . . this will happen with anyone you get involved with. You have to work on it to keep it strong."

"I know, but I don't want to. I don't see myself married to you for my whole life, my first and last! I don't want to hurt you, but I have to be true to myself."

Truth to oneself—another unassailable trump card. "But I . . . But . . . you *did* desire me," I stammered, scrambling for some kind of partial credit.

"Yes . . . I did," he admitted. "A lot, at first."

"Well"—I tried to smile—"at least there's that." I was thrown, but I was determined to try to be a good sport. At least Teddy was honest and awkwardly present, and I aspired to be *classy*. "Look, you're really tired, and really hot, and drunk. I don't want to lose you. We can make adjustments, you just have to tell me what you need. Can't we just say you'll think about it for a couple days and see if you still feel this way?"

He paused. "Well . . ." He seemed to suspect a trick. "I guess that makes sense."

"And hey, Teddy, your future boyfriends may not treat you so well. You can always refer to me and say, 'Blue would never do that.' "

"Great, Blue. You'll be my secret weapon!" We shared a grin, the grin of real friends. "Oh, I have to go weigh myself. In all this heat I haven't eaten, and I want to see if I've lost some weight!"

He went to the bathroom to stand on the scale. I'd hoped for a tad more anguish at his end, but that's selfish of me, I guess, and, after all, I had authorized him to feel all right about it.

We talked on the phone a few days later, and I tasted hope when Teddy said, "I've felt like crap for the past three days. I miss you." We didn't get together, though, and gradually he performed the *Homeresque,* making and canceling dates like Chinese water torture. It was the same thing all over again, and, once again, it was all over me. It would have been funny if it wasn't my own fatheaded heart that had walked off the same cartoon cliff twice. I thought of what Karl Marx supposedly said, though it sounds more like Groucho—"Once is tragedy. Twice is a farce."

"I know I keep canceling on you," he finally admitted. "I have to confess, I'm scared of seeing you. You'll be unhappy, and I'll just feel awful. What I need is time to myself." All I could think was, At least he's calling me to cancel instead of standing me up or waiting for me to call when he's late and then canceling! Progress!

Still, I felt moronically like the huge cartoon sheepdog who wants a little friend in order to *hug him and squeeze him and love him and hold him* until the playmate is squashed. I felt Teddy retreating over the phone, and when I realized he really wasn't going to come back, my classiness snapped. I started to cry, which repelled him. Once you witness someone desperate, that's how you see him from then on. And I don't think Teddy'd ever witnessed anyone desperate. I remembered that he'd smashed up several cars his parents bought him—his dad owned a number of car dealerships, so replacing them was relatively simple—so maybe he wasn't used to consequences or even introspection. I tried to keep reminding myself, *We didn't actually have sex. That's not the perfect relationship. Is it?*

Finally he did come to pick up his things, but he warned me on the phone beforehand that he wouldn't speak to me while he did. Through some silent-movie dumb show, I asked him for and he let me keep his toothbrush, so I could have something of his to put to my lips. He laughed when I kissed it, but then shook his head, like *You're trying to get me to talk!*

I didn't see him for several weeks. When I bicycled past Bambino's I felt ashamed of the thrill it gave me, but proud that I didn't stop. Progress! In a gift shop I saw a kitsch porcelain figure of a disturbingly childlike bride and groom, and the groom powerfully resembled Teddy. I almost bought it, but then I realized I had no idea what it meant, and it certainly would have sent a weird message as a gift to Teddy. So, no desperation presents. Progress!

I was walking across Central Park on a hot afternoon, then, and I saw Teddy with Leo, both unsteadily coming downhill on Rollerblades. They had shaved their heads, that summer's disconcerting babes-in-boot-camp look. When Teddy saw me, he lost his balance and took a painful looking spill, and his hands and knees were bruised. "Oh fuck!" he said, struggling up, crabby and frustrated. I'd never heard him say "fuck" before.

"Teddy! Hi! Hi, Leo." I tried to be positive enough for both of us, but I knew we were firmly on the wrong track. Leo impatiently folded his arms and looked past me, a body in motion that wished to remain in motion.

"How are you?" Teddy said, without speaking my name.

"Good! Maintaining, anyway."

"Maintaining? What?" He was resisting engagement.

"Well, you know! Myself! The ol' urine machine." In my nervousness I was making inadvertently creepy jokes.

"Eew!" Teddy made a face at that image.

"Well, I'm songwriting, too." I tried to clamber back into normality. "The yearning machine." Again, wrong idea.

"Good for you." He let the silence stretch. And Leo looked at him to resume their skating. I tried to cram in my affection before they moved on.

"It's great to see you!"

"Don't start, now."

"I'm just telling you how I feel."

Leo rolled his eyes and whispered into Teddy's ear, again, the schoolboys versus the teacher. Teddy giggled at whatever it was Leo said. The contempt of it made me involuntarily angry, like being pushed.

"Teddy!"

"Oh, good grief. I'm sorry, okay? I can't ever see you without having to apologize!"

"But we were close!"

"You and your broken record broken heart! I'm sick of explaining that I can't explain it! Stop harassing me for reasons!"

"Don't be angry! Why are you angry?"

"Why are you? I'm tired! You know what I realized? I only stayed with you because I needed to get out of my crowded apartment!" Oh no, I was Ellen's Xenon, an old guy with a roomy house. "Now I realize, Blue. I never loved you."

"Please don't say that. You don't have to love me now, but you did once."

"I just *thought* I did."

"But isn't that the same thing?"

"Oh, that's right! You're always right and I'm always wrong! Boo Hoo Blue! All you do is make me feel bad!"

I should never have told him about George calling me Boo Hoo. I felt bad that he felt bad to see me, but he was blaming me for his feeling guilty. "But haven't I tried to be a good sport about this? Haven't I been classy?"

"Who cares, Blue? *Who cares?*"

The Manhattan poison had taken effect. Pinocchio and Lampwick on Pleasure Isle. I tried to summon reasons to dismiss him, I remembered Nathan calling him a brat, but there was that beautiful home-at-last mouth, those guileless eyes, and that soft, Olympic shaven nape. *Beauty Fool!* And there was sneering Leo, offering immoral support. I guess it had been a love triangle, and the best friend had won. Leo grinned at me like the devil in those *Twilight Zone* fade-outs where they take you to hell on a technicality. Something cracked, and I yelled at Teddy. "You *said* you loved me! At least treat me like a human being!"

A few passing strangers eyed me with concern, and I imagine pitied the stunned, soft-faced boys staring at me. It had not been classy, but my outburst was pride's sneeze, hydraulically necessary. I felt the ground open beneath me—not only had I just volunteered to be the Elephant Man in his eyes from then on but I had made somehow sure that he would dread seeing or talking to me in the future. I was never again going to see his face light up at the sight of mine, and the certitude gripped me like a death warrant I had mistakenly signed instead of a peace treaty.

I tried to steer away from the cliff. "Teddy, you have to understand, I don't want to be angry, but love isn't allowed to go quietly! You'll understand in time!"

"That's right, you know everything, and I'm the fool! At this moment, I hate you."

"You can't mean that! It's puppy hate! You'll outgrow it!"

"Well . . ." He pouted. "I don't want to talk to you for a long, long time."

I'd made a scene, so he was somehow the Kindly One for commuting my death sentence to life with possible parole, and now I had to take the Ceremonial Walk of Guilt. When you're the one being rejected, there's no way you can be right.

As I walked away, Leo called after me, "You're just too *old!*" Oh no, I was Xenon again. Or worse, a lonesome monster, Dracula, no, make that Frankenstein. I don't dress well enough for Dracula. The Phantom of the Square Dance. *Maw, Bigfoot's out by the swing set again!*

With Homer, the sting in the farewell kiss had been Success Triumphant. After all these years, this was more biologically terrorizing Youth Triumphant. Heedless, smooth Teddy and Leo had decades of admirers and fun to look forward to, but I was a drowning, unaccompanied, pasty guy, going down for the third time. Well, the second time. I get to drown one more time. Is that hope?

When I phoned Red about losing Teddy, he said, "Blue, at that age even straight people are moving targets. He doesn't even know who he is yet." And, by my calculations, gay people start mentally healthy dating about seven years after everyone else. So I was being thrown over by someone who, in Love Years, was only fifteen.

Red went on, and cited the Homer moment. "In every romance there's a Yike point, you hit the wall, you realize that with that profound depth there's an abyss. When you take a life in your hands, it inevitably reminds you, life is headed for death, and you blame your lover. This kid never encountered that, so rather than pass through it, he's run from it. He'll know better next time. You made him comfortable with intimacy, and he can love the next one." Great, I was Teddy's discarded training wheels, his uncompleted workload from Beginning Love.

I went to a dinner party the next night—I was eager for some distraction to pre-empt my inner TV program, *Teddy's New Face*. Everyone else seemed to be relaxed, but the conversation made me tremble. One married couple referred to marriage as Endless Mutual Baby-sitting, and when I pointed out that good baby-sitters aren't having sex with their charges, she laughed. "Neither are we!" Everyone else found this a merry zinger, but I chose to be chilled. The married woman breezily observed that if she'd put a penny in a bowl every time she and her husband had had sex in the first year of their marriage, and then removed a penny every time they had sex after that, the bowl would never be emptied. Again, everyone laughed, but maybe her Brooklyn accent made it all seem bouncier.

That night I dreamed I was having actual sex with Teddy, but my thrusting made everything shake, and I realized we were on a precarious upper girder of what was either the skeleton of a decaying old building or the unsteady frame of an unfinished new one, and gorgeous green hillsides stretched out beneath us dangerously. I immediately stopped trying to force him, because the important thing was for the building not to collapse, for us to survive.

24 : PROGRESS!

I heard Reed was gravely ill and went to see him in the hospital. He was in the same room Lloyd had had. I was about to lean on his side table to greet him when he grew uncharacteristically animated. "Oo, careful! Don't sit on the goatherd!"

One of his friends had brought Reed several of his Hummel figures from his apartment, and they seemed to peer around the medicine vials and tissue boxes on his side table. The porcelain babes in the plastic wood.

"You just missed my parents. They have been so great through all this, and so have my friends. I'm pretty lucky. I mean, besides the dying part."

I asked Reed what was wrong with him. He crossed his eyes like he was tired of telling people, then started to recite his maladies, opportunistic infections with acronyms like TNT and PDQ, but he spoke so helpfully and brightly, it was like he was pushing the beverage cart up the plane aisle and announcing the drink options to the passengers: *I have this and this and this and also, this.*

"Oh Reed, I wish I had magical powers," I responded helplessly.

The matronly British volunteer whom Lloyd had routed came in and asked, "How's everything?"

Reed smiled at her. "I can't account for *everything,* but I myself am fine!"

"Oh that's super!" She beamed and sailed out of the room to recite further ritual cheer elsewhere.

"I had to tell her I was fine," he confided. "She gets so unhappy and confused if you say anything else! So, how's your own case history? Where's your little Hummel figure?"

"I wish he were that simple, Reed, but he's not. He needed some time away from me. Like, the rest of his life. I'm very sad about it . . ." My voice trailed off, suddenly aware I was complaining to someone on his deathbed about my Prom Trouble.

"Well . . . You know what they say, Blooey. Experience is the ability to recognize a mistake—when you make it again!" He stirred in bed, and I could tell he was trying not to exhibit pain. He sighed and continued, "The worst part is when they return their set of keys, isn't it?"

"Oh my gosh! He never returned his set of keys!" I realized.

"So he could sneak back into your bed!" He grinned.

"Please don't tease me, Reed," I said.

"Well then, he could sneak in and kill you!"

"I don't think he cares enough to kill me now." There was a pause, the kind hospitals specialize in, as white as the room.

Reed's eyes glittered in his wizened face. "Oh gee, that's too bad!"

We laughed, and then Reed grimaced at some sudden pang. "It's like that old doctor joke—'Only when I laugh.' " He groaned again. "I'm really tired," he confessed. "Too tired to panic anymore . . ." He took a careful breath. "Unless you like watching me try to sleep, I'd say the pj party's run its course. I'll see you soon—well, assuming I can still see. We'll . . . oh, we'll split some morphine."

He closed his eyes, clearly proud of his ability to joke. It impressed me that Reed was as nervous as a mouse about little things, like his figurines, but as stoic as a mouse about his mortality. I had to learn from him about bearing my more imaginary burdens with more reason. When he and his pain got worse, and he didn't recognize me, I allowed myself to stop visiting. I was Teddy to his me. That's why I'd resisted involvement in the first place. Deathbeds are difficult as a way of life.

Now Reed's flying the friendly skies without an airplane. His older brother, a full-fledged pilot, scattered his ashes during free fall of a parachute jump, while their identically old parents clutched each other in bewilderment below.

After that rich Gershwin interlude with Teddy, the band had switched back to lean country-western again. And this time, all my friends were dead or out of town. For the first time, it hit me that I had no parents to turn to, and no children to live for. I had to take slow, deep breaths to avoid that pang of abandonment that so adores rushing into a vacuum. Sweet, semisolid Teddy needed to grow, and I had to have the self-control to stay out of his way. As long as I could avoid hearing "My Old Kentucky Home" or "Red River Valley."

Still, although I tried to defer it, I crashed again, unexpectedly doomed twice, and once again clambered through panics about time's rapid-fire delivery. I'd gone from Boo Hoo to Big Shoe to Beast, from mere to mighty to moot; from flowing, blue-eyed Earth to shriveling, hulky Mars. Without Teddy in my arms, I felt like an amputee. But at least not a quadruple amputee this time, just a double amputee. I could still walk. Progress!

Passing Bambino's I got a rabbit punch of nostalgia. Teddy and his places and props had become legends to me or, anyway,

magical plot points in my own saga, just like Dad's precinct headquarters and Mom's desk at the library, or even Homer's collection of clumsily hewn angels. The Home of the Fried Ravioli
Basket should be a mundane spot to me, but it seemed charged
with kinetic hope, inaccessible hope, like a clue to a rebus whose
code, once cracked, would spill happiness like the contents of a
piñata onto me, the Left Out party kid. At least I was relieved to
realize that my grief over Teddy had replaced my sorrow over
Homer. It's like a Magic Slate, or an Etch-A-Sketch! You can't be
heartbroken over two loves at the same time! Progress!

I thought I'd get a physical or do my overdue taxes as
penance, but it turned out my doctor—of the sharp suits and the
leather harness—and even my accountant had both recently died.
So, too, I heard, had Alden Powers, who'd seemed as solid as Fort
Knox the last time I'd seen him. Then I read that Fritz Middling
had died, and it reminded me that old people die, too. *I have my
health,* I repeated as a mantra, and this time I didn't even consider
suicide. Progress! I'd never commit suicide, it would hurt Red.
He's my safety net.

As I clutched my mind's seat handles, waiting for the turbu-
lence to pass, and this time knowing it would, my mild neighbor
Alice again asked me to place some anonymous phone calls for
her, and it turned out this time it wasn't over a reluctant pool
player. She was helplessly in love with a married man who'd
stopped calling her, and she wanted to find out if he'd separated
from his wife as he'd promised to. "Just find out if he's there and
then hang up!" Wow. Everybody is totally nuts, not just me. That's
a comfort. If not Progress.

25 : COOKIE FUMES

The seasons pass faster all the time, the sun and moon alternate like a strobe light. Beggars' Night, Halloween, All Souls', Thanksgiving. Thanksgiving is the first warning sign of Christmas. And Christmas came up on me from behind last year, that bejeweled, lumbering juggernaut, that deep-soaked byzantine denial of midwinter, worse than television commercials for prettily pressuring the beholder to be coupled and cozy. One icy night, maddened by cookie fumes from a neighboring apartment (Alice baking for her, as it were, husband?), I couldn't resist calling Teddy—my Telemachus the Pale-Skinned, Onetime Bringer of Cookies

"I just wanted to see how you are . . ."

He was blank, but cordial anyway He'd reduced my sentence. "Fine. I haven't done a thing about getting a real job. I get so tired, you know that. I saw you playing piano on the *Entertainment Tonight* piece about Randy."

"Whoa, sharp eye! And how's your visual? Still hypershort hair-wise?"

"It was too harsh. I stopped getting tips. So I let it grow back. I look innocent again. And they're tipping again!"

"And are you traveling home for Christmas?"

"No, I'm spending it in Connecticut with a friend."

That old, pointedly vague tip-off. "I get it. Won't your parents miss you?"

"No, I saw them at Thanksgiving. I told them I was gay."

"That's great! I'm so proud of you! How did you do it?"

"Well, my mom asked if I was gay and I said yes."

"And I'll bet that's cool with them."

"Oh, sure. My mom did say it was a sin, though, and that she knew some men who had prayed to Jesus to change them, and they were happily married now. It's all fine, though."

"Eventually people will have to see that it's a part of nature, like green eyes and left-handedness."

"They will. My mom asked if I was still seeing you."

"Smart woman. What did you tell her?"

"I said now and then, no big deal."

Though this sounded better than I was actually getting, it depressed me. "And this new guy?"

"He's not glamorous like you. He's a waiter, too."

I didn't know if that was his job or his erotic status. "I'd love to meet him," I said, not even sounding convincing to myself.

"I'll bet. He says he never, ever wants to meet you."

So at least I was still seen as a threat. That felt good, for some reason. "I hope he treats you right."

"He's a jerk. We fight all the time. He says I don't satisfy him. But I don't have to be careful of his feelings, and he lives in Connecticut, so I only have to see him once a week. He has his own washer-dryer, though."

"Is that good, fighting all the time? You deserve someone kind."

He groaned. "I know, like *you*. Well, he's more of a challenge."

"Well, I challenged you sometimes."

"You'll always have an answer, won't you? Fine, let's just say I needed to see the world. I don't know what I want. New subject."

"How's Leo?"

"Insane. He's hung up on this sixteen-year-old busboy at work who isn't even gay. Oh, he took me to a sex club last week, BAIT, have you heard of it?"

"No . . ." Actually, I had, but even at this point-of-no-returned-love I still wanted to buff my image as a decent guy.

"It is really seedy, it's hilarious. We were only supposed to watch, but Leo was drunk and got carried away."

"Please, Teddy, promise me you'll be careful."

"You're talking like an old man again."

"Well, I care about you. You're a sweet guy."

"Thanks." I waited for a return mollifier, but Teddy summoned up an artificially flowering hedge of chat. "I'm going to Miami for a week in January."

"With this guy?"

"No!" He giggled, as if that were laughable. "I'm going with some of the would-be models from work. Miami is a big modeling spot right now."

I didn't have any modeling insights to offer, so I tried to re orient the conversation, that is, toward sentimental reminders that we had in fact shared some beautiful depths. "How's the golden twig silverware?"

"Well, you know what? I had a dinner party using them, and . . . they are awfully hard to hold."

I remembered that he had never made me that fancy dinner he promised me, but I figured it wouldn't be classy to bring it up. I should have let go at this point, but the loss still rattled me. "Oh Teddy . . ." I began, and the unexpected longing in my voice was toxic to him.

"It's still over, Blue," he recited, his voice already driving into the distance. "When all is said and done . . . All is said and done. I've got to go, I've got a chicken baking."

I tried the old bond-by-humor. "Well, baking chickens wait for no man!"

"No, Blue. They don't. Happy new year!"

I imagined his soft face—Beauty Fool!—and went out for a walk on Riverside Drive. In the moonlit—rare for Manhattan—street outside my building, the freezing wind was pushing an empty soda can around in jerky half circles, like a remote-controlled toy run by an indecisive, invisible child. It had the pathos of a floundering fish and seemed to follow me as I headed across to the park itself. The glittering lacework vaulting of black branches seemed to form gleaming circular webs where the moon passed behind them. The solemn black floor of river, the decorous-by-distance lights of New Jersey, all were as bracing as when Homer and I, and Teddy and I, had walked there. Why did I feel a weight in my stomach and a vise clinching my throat? The moon endlessly recites the secrets of the universe in a very clear voice, except that it's in a language we don't understand.

I turned onto a side street, and there were the mysterious, comforting stained-glass windows of the Upper West Side townhouses, the deadpan carved lion heads over the wrought-iron doorways, the comfort of home with the mystique of a church, the comfort of church and the mystique of home. These were as eye-filling as ever. Why were they insufficient now? Did I feel the need for a co-witness because I was so used to it, with my eagle-eyed twin and crowd of friends and family? Or was it because I was so isolated, despite all that company? Would heterosexuality have made any difference in my sense of belonging? Had I actually shared more than most people, or been more alone? I couldn't figure it out, and I cursed the fact that the splendor and brilliant meaninglessness of this icy night were not enough for me.

A few weeks later, I was standing on the subway platform and a young couple walked past me—cute college kids, in matched denim jackets, and his arm was wrapped around hers. The only odd thing were the scratch marks all over his face. Had they fought and made up, or was there an extramarital explanation? Maybe he'd wrassled a puma in her defense. Before I could consider the options, I suddenly saw Leo. After initially standoffish chat, and an announced long delay in the train's arrival, we warmed up to each other—at least New York's inconvenience gives everyone common bonds—and, anyway, the situation obliged us to talk. He half-joked about a sexually illegible NYU freshman he was pursuing.

"Can you believe it, the kid thinks I'm too old for him!"

There was no benefit for me to follow that line, so I brought up Teddy.

"We both love the guy, that should make us allies," I plugged away.

Leo shrugged. "Fine. I'm concerned about Frat Brother Fife, though. He's aimless, and he just lets himself be taken care of. You know how easily swayed he is!" I didn't know if I'd been criticized or not.

"What is this new guy like?" I asked. You always think knowledge of the new lover will somehow teach you about yourself.

Leo made a hateful face. As handsome as he was, when he frowned he looked like the cranky old neighbor who phones the police when you cut across his lawn. "I have a deep, deep disdain for him, for reasons I am not going to go into with you here." The Homer Winger School of Announced but Unexplained Hatred. "Teddy's just settling for the guy. God bless him! Anyhoo, where the hell are you going in a necktie?"

"I'm having a probably pointless business lunch at Que Sera Sera."

"Teddy and I are going there on Friday night. To check out a *real* Italian restaurant! Without Whatsisname. Teddy gets every Friday night off."

"Off?" I said. "You make his relationship sound like a job."

Leo gazed heavenward like the cat on trial for eating the canary. "I'm not going to comment there. For starters, though, this guy is even older than you! Teddy's always selling himself short." He didn't seem to realize he'd insulted me. At least Lloyd never hurt my feelings accidentally.

Leo smiled secretively. "It can't last. I have absolute faith in that."

26 : LAST LICKS

Down in SoHo in search of Ho Ho, I ran into Phizz, who was walking his latest dog, an unwieldy husky that kept straining its leash.

"Down, Dad, down!" Phizz's command was weak, despite his biceps. "The name was Homer's idea. He said I should call it Dad just to see how people react when I call him in the park. *Here, Dad!* It's funny, people get all weird. I've met a couple guys that way. Don't tell Derek. I mean, I just *meet* them."

"I don't even know Derek," I put in helpfully.

"Well, he's always off somewhere, isn't he?" Phizz paused and then added, "By the way, Our Mr. Winger has just gotten out of the hospital."

Oh no, not this—

"I don't know about what, but as far as I know I don't think he's in any pain. There was this big, mean guy he was seeing who was into some pretty rough stuff, so I don't know if it's like, injuries, or just ordinary illness, you know?"

Hearing about Homer's sex life so blandly from Phizz bewildered me—my heart's own as distant gossip, my sacred temple as public phone booth. "Is there anything else I should know, Phizz?"

"Not that I can think of. . . . Oh, yes! His loft is in *Architectural Digest* this month!"

I felt I had to check in with Homer, though whether it was penis, heart, or brain that rallied me, you tell me. To my surprise, I couldn't remember his phone number—Progress!—and had to look it up in the phone book. I found it on the page that goes from Wine to Winter. He'd changed it in moving, anyhow. When I called him, he was friendly, as he'd been at our last encounter, and it turned out he just had gone in for a checkup, and dizzy Phizz misreported it.

"I finally took the HIV test, Blue. I know you always wanted me to, but first I made a huge donation to AIDS research. *Huge.* I guess I was trying to bribe God. But hey, it worked! I'm negative!"

Homer said he'd been seeing a wealthy German businessman—his phrase. Was this the mean guy Phizz mentioned? But now the affair had collapsed, and I wondered if our mutually broken hearts could make us easier-going friends now. Again, I suppose my Iago penis was secretly brainwashing me to believe my compulsions were actually good intentions.

He invited me to see his new apartment in TriBeCa, and I went. It was a vast loft, a kingdom, where his other place had been an enchanted hut. It was full of beautiful antiques, though muted and casually arranged, no swag or gilding—as Lloyd would say, friendly enough to avoid charges of perfection. Instead of the small wooden saints, great, weathered, life-size—if that word is applicable here—gray stone statues of Christ and Buddha and Shiva loomed in corners, surrounded by bowls of fresh flowers. The saints, after all, were just underlings compared to these guys.

"Not too fancy-schmancy?" he asked as he led me in.

"No, it's fancy, but it avoids schmancy."

He told me he'd just bought a sports car, a Testarossa. "I think it translates as Big Red Scrotum!" He laughed, tossing his briefcase on a leather couch.

Somehow, in changing from his business suit to casual clothes, Homer emerged in just his briefs to chat with me and, Clean Plate Club champion that I am, I again headed for the salt lick, and we ended up making out. Swept back into the elusive passion that had become as mythical to me as Orpheus tailing Eurydice, I dizzied at the cushioned, milky taste of the impossible, like time travel on my lips. Homer grinned and whispered, "Big Shoe . . . I remember this . . . mmmm . . . so well." I tried to mentally record the sensation, the way a camel drinks up before re-entering the desert. Finally, though not immediately, Homer broke away and pulled on some jeans. We resumed chatting as if nothing had happened, and that was his right, and it was what I expected.

We sized each other up for a minute. "Ohhhh . . . I have to tell you, Blue, after all this time . . . ," he began significantly. "Just . . . Well . . . I have trouble talking about my problems. It's not all my fault, the way I act. I didn't graduate from college like I said. I wanted you to be impressed with me. I didn't even go to high school. I had to listen hard and pick things up as I went. My family doesn't have a ranch. Shit, I lived in a car for a year. My father wasn't a nuclear scientist. I wanted you to think I was smart. I don't even know who he was. Some cowboy my mom picked up."

So, not a scientist, not abusive, not dead, just unknown?

"And . . . the things she subjected me to. . . . She was a whore. She denies it now, but she was. Didn't even bother to close her door half the time. And when she didn't have a man around, she'd abuse me, she'd force me to do things. . . . You can't imagine. It's not all my fault."

So, not good, not vanished, not dead? I didn't even know what to visualize here, and at this point I wasn't even going to guess what the real truth was. I just assumed whatever it was, it was sad. Was there any point in saying I would have loved him no matter what?

"I thought you had foster parents," I said in my confusion. I forgot who'd told me what about him.

"What? Who told you that?" He became agitated.

I thought of the spectral man at the Deep End, and couldn't bear to bring him up. "I don't— It must have been one of your Fire Island friends."

"Those people aren't my friends," he said. "You should never have talked about me to them." Anyway, the phone rang and Homer disappeared to talk on it. "It's important business from Japan!" At least he explained it this time. At least I felt more comfortably ridiculous at this replay of old dynamics, and not heart-wrung. It was all so intensely the same. It was more the same than ever. And no matter my desires, I'd finally exhausted every emotion with Homer but forgiveness. And at this late date, my ex-loves had turned and turned like an excessively twisted Möbius strip, and I gave up trying to know which side of the ribbon was the real one.

27 : ALL FOR NOW

Red and Jeannie, that Dope and Dopess, got married in Santa Fe, her family's favorite vacation spot. Red had suggested Las Vegas, but it isn't truly classy, Sinatra or not, and, as Jeannie pointed out, "It would be as if you're telling everyone you're not really serious."

The church was a small, whitewashed adobe, simple and airy, decorated with comical sad *santos* figures like Homer's. It was Catholic, but blessedly unlike the dark battleship wine cellar of St. Vitus's, and the timeless horizon outside the open windows offered me a humbling perspective. *Mountains come and go, the stars disperse, the oceans retreat. Will the little gay speck in that clay structure find a date?*

On the way to the inn for the reception, Ellen, who hadn't been in a church in years, told me—as if it was a scandal—that George, after years of no longer attending Mass, had resumed going since his retirement. "And he goes *every day*," she whispered, "when it's not even a sin not to." She smiled out at the desert, at the molecule-shaped cacti, and at the mountains named for the Blood of Christ. "Nearer my God to thee?"

Watching the ethereal landscape roll by, I was reminded that on life's auto ride, in the sunshine of good fortune, all you see is the passing countryside. Only in bad times, in a dark tunnel or at night, do you see your own face reflected back at you in the window, and that's when you get a chance to appraise who you are yourself.

The reception was held in the courtyard of an old inn, with a modestly plashing tile fountain demonstrating serenity for the newlyweds. I felt uplifted by the event and the presence of movie stars and family. Kitty was on Cloud Ten, of course, to meet Atom Boy, as well as all the actors from *Here's How!* and she dutifully explained to them the plots of the episodes they'd starred in. In the cleansing sunlight of the plaza, even spiritually waterlogged Sean looked bright and upbeat, and Bridge-out beamed that her protegé had won a race. Red had jumped off the garage and landed on his feet.

As the festivity wound down, and people could sit and shoot the breeze rather than rush to catch up, Red told me he'd gotten his first movie role. "An action flick. Lots of explosions!" He grinned. And the equivalent of Nazis, I assume. "I play the supporting lead, the lovable cop who gets killed. Blue, isn't that a lifelong dream?"

At the reception's end, dictated by the Great Party Planner as nightfall, all the children untied and released the decorative helium balloons, which rose and dispersed in the desert night, a mix of loss and exaltation, and, frankly, aerial littering.

"Mmmm! The desert is so beautiful," tiny Belinda announced solemnly, gazing out the entryway and stretching her arms in a rapturous gesture she must have seen on television. Already a little contestant.

"Yes!" Red called to her, adopting her beatific tone while he clutched Jeannie in the quickly chilling dark. "Just watch out for the scorpions, tarantulas, and rattlers!"

Belinda squeaked and ran back inside.

. . .

That night I dreamed I went back to the old house in Cleveland to visit Mom, and to tell her about the wedding. She was young, healthy-looking, and enthusiastic, and even Dad was there, young as Mom was, like in Ellen's home movies, cracking jokes and repeating, "I thought they were gonna keep me down there forever!" They were happy to hear the details of the reception, how nobody took a swing at anybody, and Mom patted Dad's arm and said, "It's nice to have the old fella back home, I can tell you!" The furniture and walls were all overgrown with vines and vegetation, like a lost city, birds were flying around inside the house, and, idyllically, deer were grazing on the roof. Mom explained that, since we were all grown, they were going to raise animals now to make extra money.

At last, being alone is as normal as love had seemed while it was going on. It all has to do with time ratios. Maybe I keep mistaking the Easy for the Deep. I guess I have to get used to the possibility of Paradise Lost on a regular basis. Shangri-la is rezoned as the Land of No Can Do. At least Homer and Teddy, and, hey, while we're at it, music, were my stints of ecstasy, my Fresh Air Funds on a smoggy planet, summer homes with hidden structural damage, joy inevitably touched by fear, but joy nonetheless. Well, Eternal Coach, Manager of All Teams, I tried. And music will always be mine.

So, there's my Classic Comics Illustrated *My Two False One True Loves*. Boy finds love, Boy loses love, Boy finds seemingly far truer love, Boy loses that, too. At this point, Boy isn't a boy anymore. With neither parents nor children to define me as child or parent, I amble on, no breakthroughs, no breakdowns, ever upward and downward. Time Marches Funny. You want life to be a fable, or a legend, but it's an epic shaggy dog story. And I'm just one more grizzling spear carrier in that overproduced and unfocused Grand Opera Earth.

I've come to the exactly-half-hopeful conclusion that I got it backward on that lyric I wrote at age eleven. Life Is the Answer, and it's Love That's the Question. After loving and losing once, I thought my life was over. But if it can happen to me twice, two points chart a line—it can happen to me a third time. And even then, I'll know there are no happy endings. Only happy chapters. And there's sure no table of contents. Love is the all-time box-office champ and most-publicized mystery. That's why they keep writing songs trying to figure it out. And even figuring it out wouldn't change anything, just like solving a murder doesn't bring back the dead, or understanding Halley's comet doesn't affect its rarity. Anyway, it's always been pretty clear where life is headed. Love is the part that's hard to chart.

Last night I went to see Milla at the Keyboard Room. Now that she's used to the thrill of her son enough to leave him with baby-sitters, she's gone back to the cabaret circuit. She's had her long, wild hair cut in a sleek pageboy, and someone decided she was incomparable, so she has all the work she wants—that long, tall vulnerability of hers offsets her evening gowns nicely. I sat with her Russell, the sound man in both senses. By the end of the evening she seemed relaxed, as if singing Jerome Kern had unburdened her of a painful secret.

"This last song is by a friend of mine. He's a songwriting fool, but he's my kind of fool. Blue—I wish you Ithaca." The audience's silence read as confusion. "Not the city upstate," she added nervously. "I mean, you know, *home.*

> *A rose is picked, and soon it dies.*
> *It never could be otherwise.*
> *But heaven knows, that rose, it tries.*
> *That's all I know for now—*
> *It's all for now.*

The thrill may come, but it will go.
It hurts me some, but I don't know. . . .
It's worth the wait to join the show.
That's all I know for now—
It's all for now.

Love's never here.
It just passes by.
The cheek with a tear
tomorrow is dry.

Time won't explain,
it just goes ahead.
Just like the rain.
Just like I said,

You'd think that I'd be getting wise.
Well, love at least is exercise.
And heaven knows, that rose, it tries.
That's all I know,
it's all for now.
That's all for now.

A NOTE ON THE TYPE

The text of this book was set in film in a typeface named Bembo. The roman is a copy of a letter cut for the celebrated Venetian printer Aldus Manutius by Francesco Griffo. It was first used in Cardinal Bembo's *De Aetna* of 1495—hence the name of the revival. Griffo's type is now generally recognized, thanks to the research one of Stanley Morison, to be the first of the old-face group of types. The companion italic is an adaptation of the chancery script type designed by the Roman calligrapher and printer Lodovico degli Arrighi, called Vincentino, and used by him during the 1520s.

Composed by North Market Street Graphics,
Lancaster, Pennsylvania

Printed and bound by R. R. Donnelley & Sons,
Harrisonburg, Virginia

Typography and binding design
by Dorothy S. Baker